D0838747

The Room with Closets
TALES OF A LIFE DIVIDED

A. Pablo Iannone

Vagabond Press
~ out there but hard to find ~

Earlier versions of four of the stories in this book appeared as follows:

"The Room with Closets," under the title "El cuarto de los placares," in the Argentine electronic publication *Textos de la Víspera* (June 20, 2002).

"Batata's Flight," under the title "El vuelo de Batata," in *Textos de la Víspera* (August 2, 2001).

"Margarita's Wedding," under the title "El casamiento de Margarita," in *Textos de la Víspera* (November 15, 2001). An earlier English version of this story was awarded Honorable Mention in the Mainstream/Literary Short Story category of the 1998 *Writer's Digest* Writing Competition.

"South," in Fernando Alegría and Alberto Ruffinelli (eds.) *Paradise Lost or Gained? The Literature of Hispanic Exile* (Houston: Arte Público, 1990).

Published by

Vagabond Press

Cover design by Travis Weller

First Edition
Printed in the United States of America

Library of Congress Control Number 2006920334
ISBN-10   0-9755716-3-X
ISBN-13   978-0-9755716-3-7

Vagabond Press
P.O. Box 4830
Austin, TX   78765
vagabondpress.com

To my entire family, North and South, who give stability
to my present and hope to my future.

The events and characters in these stories are as real as the author's
memories—constrained by his ignorance and the passing of time; and as
unreal as the author's fantasies—constrained by his experience and the
limits of his imagination. It is up to the curious to determine the right
mixture of reality and appearance in them.

Contents

The Room with Closets
TALES OF A LIFE DIVIDED

A. Pablo Iannone

EVOCATIONS

The Room with Closets

Ignacio José Conti had the good and the bad luck of being born of poor parents—the experience was instructive, but not always worth the accompanying pain. He also had the good and the bad luck of growing up while his parents slowly made a small fortune— his schooling was excellent, though not always capable of moderating his impatient dreams.

The seeming ambivalence of his situation did not, however, end there. As an adolescent in cosmopolitan Buenos Aires, Ignacio was continually faced with other worlds, fantastic or foreign, in the midst of the harsh economic and political realities of Argentina during the 1950's. These recurring clashes of mind and world eventually caused him to develop an inveterate feeling of claustrophobia. In fact, when he was sixteen, Ignacio began to experience an overwhelming need to escape—from *what* he did not know.

Around that time, his parents, motivated by duty and the desire to provide a better life for their children as much as by the seductions of prosperity, overcame the modesty and the inertia that tied them up to their small rented apartment in Villa Pueyrredón—a Buenos Aires neighborhood remarkable for its great people, not its great wealth— and allowed themselves the luxury of buying an immense house in Almagro, a more elegant area of the city.

They did not plan to occupy it for a while; but Ignacio, fascinated by its silences and its echoes and wishing to become, however partially, independent from his parent's tutelage, could not wait. He brought a mattress, a table, a chair, and a few other things to establish himself in the place.

The house was full of surprises. Each step opened a door—to a room, a patio, a corridor, a staircase, a mystery. But the mystery of all mysteries was the room with closets. It was on the second floor and very small. Doors of various shapes and sizes almost entirely covered its walls. Only the halves of two walls were visible. Where they touched, there was a hollowed out rectangular section. It was narrow and about a foot and a half deep. At its end, a little window opened to the tall gray walls above a small and dark inside patio that offered silence to the ground floor.

Ignacio did not have any trouble getting used to the house, even though it was somewhat difficult to learn how to find one's way around it at night (there were at most three light bulbs in the place). He did not install any others, however, because he both liked the darkness and he had no money.

His preference for the darkness was as ingrained as his rather compulsive habit of locking doors. He had displayed this disposition since early childhood, when he also used to run with blue or red pencils towards the closest lock, break their leads in it, and then admire the kaleidoscopic results of his handy work through the keyhole.

Whether out of fear of being alone, or because he had never before had so many doors at his disposal, his door-locking habit strengthened soon after he moved into the house. Perhaps it was in an attempt to organize the world around him (in sealed compartments and to prevent any uncontrolled transition or disorder) that Ignacio made certain he did not miss any door, especially the one at the entrance to the room with closets, which he locked with a double twist of the key every night before going to sleep.

This compulsion was also in evidence at the beginning of each day, when Ignacio, delighting in the pleasure of his apparent independence, took advantage of the opportunity to verify once more that everything was in order in the simple and undaunted world of subdivisions and locks. One morning, however, while going through this ritual, he noticed to his surprise (and dismay) that the entrance door to the room with closets was unlocked.

Who had opened it? Not thieves. For he examined the whole house and nothing was missing. Besides, the entrance gate, the doors to the back lawn, and all the other doors were locked. What thief would have taken the trouble to lock them all when leaving? Perhaps some member of his family had entered the house while he was asleep and had left without waking him up. It seemed implausible; but just in case, he made a telephone call to the Villa Pueyrredón apartment where his family was still living. His sister, Marta, answered. Somewhat puzzled by Ignacio's question, she assured him that no member of the family had visited the new house since he had moved in.

He had absolutely no reason to doubt his sister's reply, and consequently continued his attempts to solve the mystery. Could he have opened the door while sleepwalking? No one had ever told him that he had shown any signs of somnambulism. He could not figure out what had happened.

Ignacio was still trying to explain this arcane occurrence to himself when Marta showed up at the front door. Puzzled by the story (and perhaps worried about her brother's sanity), she had come to see what was going on. He told her what he knew and what he had considered. She suggested an experiment: she would lock him up in his room that night and would leave the house with all the other doors locked as well. If the door to the room with closets was found unlocked in the morning, someone or something else would have had to unlock it.

Anxious to understand what had happened and to bring order back into his world, Ignacio soon became intrigued by the idea, and that very night, accomplices of science and madness, brother and sister began the experiment. He retired to his room on the first floor, and she went home leaving him locked up, at the mercy of fears and fires.

According to plan, Marta returned the next day and set him free. They immediately headed to the mysterious room. They found the door—not just unlocked—but wide open. Brother and sister checked the house from top to bottom. Everything else was in order. They looked at each other without understanding. "Do you believe in ghosts, brother?" asked Marta with a smile both mischievous and surprised. She added: "I don't; but it seems they do exist . . ."

Ignacio could not—nor did he want to—believe what he had seen. Marta shrugged her shoulders and left, both from fear of ghosts and the desire to gossip about the matter. "I'll come back tomorrow. My regards to *Sombrita*," she said while leaving. Whoever or whatever was unlocking the door already had a name.

Preferring the perfect disorder of the streets in Buenos Aires to the imperfect order of his recent dwelling, Ignacio left the house, too. A carnival of street vendors and tireless merry-go-rounds was dancing in his eyes. A nightmare of misplaced concepts and ungraspable geometries was choking his mind. He walked through the city until his forgetfulness calmed his uneasiness.

With dull thoughts and aching feet, he returned to the house at 10:00 p.m. Once inside, he made sure that the mysterious door was locked, and sat down right in front of it with a desk lamp on. No door was unlocked in the house. The hours went by. Nothing happened. He was about to fall asleep, when suddenly the key turned with a creaking sound. His heart jumped out of his chest and he jumped onto his feet. He felt a lump in his throat. He waited, breathless, oppressed by the indecisiveness of silence and suspense rather than by the fear of the unknown. All was quiet. He entered the room and did not find a soul—not even in the closets.

He locked it again and went to his room, where for the first time since his move, he did not lock the door. Neither locks nor compulsions could hide his vulnerability. The time was 4:00 a.m.

Exhausted, he tried to sleep, but failed. The brusque honks of the night traffic, the anguished sirens of lonely ambulances, the persistent clickety-clack of unending cargo trains, the tired step of a cart horse and the cracking cough of its owner (both condemned to carry greens to the market at dawn), the impatient howls of shadowy cats, the whistled tango of a solitary walker—all conspired to nourish his nightmares and take away his sleep. The next morning, the room with closets was still locked.

Marta returned at noon. Ignacio then told her about the new developments. Again, brother and sister went toward the room. As soon as they got to the door, the key turned by itself. They looked at each other smiling, victorious but terrified. Their astonishment had not yet left them when their mother, Josefina, showed up with her mother, Lucía Vilar, and Edelmira, an old maid from the Southern Andes who lived with them. Marta told them everything they knew.

Grandmother Lucía thought the events were the most natural thing in the world. As she said, similar happenings were an everyday occurrence in her native Spain. And she also remembered having witnessed them in the Brazilian jungle where she had spent most of her childhood. She explained that the room was inhabited by the spirit of some harmless animal, probably a pet: a dog, a canary, a parrot, or a cat. And she told them that when she was a little girl, the spirit of a monkey had eaten all the bananas they'd had for almost an entire year. Eventually, they got a pet monkey that scared the spirit away but ate half the bananas itself. Monkeys, though frequent in Villa Pueyrredón, were unlikely in the more elegant Almagro neighborhood. Maybe the ghost was a cat, given that there were so many around.

"A cat!" exclaimed Marta. "*Sombrita* is a cat! And what happens if a ghost cat has kittens? We would then be in real trouble! Invaded by a family—eventually a crowd—of invisible and mischievous cats!"

Edelmira thought differently. To her, the *Nunqueté*, the spirit of the moon, the eyes, the mirrors, and the calm lakes, inhabited the room. Someone had probably broken a mirror in the room, and the *Nunqueté* was seeking reparation.

Josefina, skeptical by nature and cautious by matrimony, believed that her daughter and son were probably suffering from hallucinations, but said that she would talk to her husband about the matter. Ignacio, at that point, would not rule out any possibilities and asked both his grandmother and the maid how they knew what they claimed. His grandmother's reasons did not go beyond, "My mother taught it to me," and "Everyone knows it." Edelmira gave no reason whatsoever. The *Nunqueté* inhabited the room and that was it. She knew.

In order to learn, as well as to attain—if not preserve—his sanity, Ignacio began to seek scientific explanations for the phenomenon. What could make the lock turn? A spring? He opened it and there was none. A magnet? There was none around. He changed the lock. The new one kept on opening by itself like the other, without apparent cause or regularity—various times one day, none another; some times at night and other times in the afternoon.

Informed of the strange events by his wife, Ignacio's father decided to deal with the matter. His name was Nicolás Conti, though people called him Colín. As it was his custom in difficult cases, he went to the venerable church of San Cayetano, the workers' patron, where he lit a candle and gave some substantial alms. He also paid a visit to a reliable *curandera* of his acquaintance.

This woman, Doña Rosa, was an old gypsy who specialized in medicinal magic, not in casting away spirits. Despite this, she would condescend to help in the case of the room with closets. She was neither indifferent to her long association with the Conti family nor to the possibility of making a few extra pesos. Her neighbors in Villa Pueyrredón respected her a great deal because, they said, she had saved the lives of many infants with her magic herbs—infants the best physicians—indeed specialists!—had given up for dead. Colín and Josefina trusted her because she had cured a few of the infant

Ignacio's attacks of indigestion with weed and toad poultices, and by pulling from his *cuerito*, the skin that covered his lower spine.

So Doña Rosa traveled to the Almagro house one afternoon, bringing along the accumulated wisdom of Egypt, Babylon, Greco-Roman antiquity, the European Middle Ages, India and the gypsies, the South American Indians, and Villa Pueyrredón—where some have argued that life began—and something like a measuring rod. Despite this ecumenical-demonological-pharmaceutical background, the woman had the most normal appearance in the world, and her general conduct did not contradict her look.

Awaiting her were Colín, Josefina, Marta, Ignacio, grandmother Lucía, Ignacio's aunt and godmother Margarita who had come to give moral support in a moment of need, Edelmira and her little niece who had tagged along out of curiosity, and a lawyer. The latter was present to advise Colín on the legality of annulling the contract by which the house had changed hands. He had invited a photographer from an evening paper who specialized in taking pictures of both flying saucers and miracles. And, of course, some neighbors from Villa Pueyrredón had also come to give support and to take gossip back to the neighborhood—to Nazca Street and the old América Avenue, where the trolleys still ran.

Marta and Ignacio led Doña Rosa (and the rest of the party) toward the mystery room. The gypsy stood in front of the door. With fast movements, the woman slid her rod through the air, along the length and the width of the closed door, as if she were drawing space in time. Subsequently, the key turned and the door opened. The lawyer muttered, *"¿Qué carajo?"* and a neighbor exclaimed, *"Cruz diablo!"* Grandmother Lucía made the sign of the cross. A small girl in the party began to cry, and her embarrassed father shouted at his wife, who picked her up. "Didn't I tell you not to bring her along? One can't bring them anywhere!" The entire time, the photographer from the newspaper continued taking pictures of everything and everyone, real or fantastic, it was possible to photograph in the place.

The gypsy was petrified. Ignacio cautiously touched the lock. Its shape was normal, and so was its temperature. When the members of the party calmed down and silence imposed itself on all once again, Doña Rosa traced other figures in the air with her rod. The door did not move. The gypsy kept on repeating this, nobody quite knowing what for, but nothing happened. Everybody looked at her inquisitively. Appearing lost in thought, she finally spoke. She said—unconvincingly—she would go home and cast away the spirits from there. She collected her fee and left.

After about four hours of heated exchanges—exchanges of theories and fantasies, everyone but Ignacio began to leave in groups, discussing the strange events of that afternoon (and other similar ones they had witnessed or heard about from a good source), relating their respective views of life, the universe, and the world beyond. They walked slowly, stopping once in a while without noticing it, toward the subways and the buses which would return them to their everyday lives.

Judging by how many times the door opened by itself after that day, Doña Rosa could not or did not keep her promise. The woman died two years later, according to the medical reports, when she became intoxicated as a consequence of ingesting a pastry which contained toxic mushrooms and other unidentified substances. The medical report totally ignored the fact that Doña Rosa had eaten the macabre concoction on the night of a full moon, which some neighbors offer as proof when they assert that Doña Rosa died a victim of love sickness or the evil eye, rather than from intoxication.

What no one disagrees with or has forgotten today in Villa Pueyrredón is the day in which Doña Rosa cast away the spirits which had invaded the mansion bought by Colín and Josefina. All of Villa Pueyrredón also acknowledges that the door to the room with closets in Almagro still keeps on opening by itself.

The participants in the events involving the room with closets have all returned to their respective lives, rather closet-style, in this multifarious universe. Ignacio and his family grew accustomed to the incomprehensible; but his curiosity never abandoned him. He pursued his investigations, and according to those who know him closely, for a while believed he had found a partial explanation of the phenomenon. Something, or someone, was producing identical electrical charges on both the lock itself and the metal plate in the doorjamb. These identical charges repelled each other, and the only part which could move withdrew, turning the key in the process. This explanation was supposedly even confirmed by experiments. Ignacio not only determined the existence but also measured the magnitude of the opposing charges produced in the lock and in the door knob.

But as he himself acknowledged, this explanation does not solve the mystery: the cause of the electrical charges is still unknown. Marta believes that it is *Sombrita* the ghost-cat. She likes the idea of a ghost-cat inhabiting the room with closets and creating electricity with its claws, but Ignacio insists that one must base one's beliefs on evidence, and that none exists to justify Marta's belief.

Grandmother Lucía, in accordance with *her* explanation, gave the family a cat, a dog, a canary, and just in case, a monkey, so that one or the other would scare away the room's ghost. The monkey escaped over a neighbor's roof and was never seen again, though it was rumored that it had ended up working at a circus in the provinces. The cat eventually ate the canary, and the dog scared away the cat but not the ghost.

Edelmira, the maid, placed a mirror in the room to appease the *Nunqueté*. It did not have any effect at all; but she never changed her mind. The *Nunqueté* inhabited the room and was seeking reparation.

Ignacio's parents never mentioned the matter again, as if they had forgotten it. As for Ignacio, he has changed, and yet, has remained the same. He gave up using his first name, Ignacio, because he read somewhere that it did not have any etymological meaning, and this emptiness bothered him. Now he uses his second name, José, because it means "he will increase" according to some—although others say it means "he will erase or take away." Be this as it may, his family still calls him Ignacio; but he is José to his friends, a situation that has caused some confusion. Indeed, there are people who wonder how the twins—Ignacio and José—can be told apart.

José has also lost the compulsion to lock doors, though he still finds it very difficult to accept imprecision, if not change. Partly as a result of his ever growing curiosity, partly because he could not control the turns of his fate, he has moved to another country where logic and mathematics are his world, and magic and gypsies belong only to literature. The facts and events of the room with closets have become nothing but a story. But this is only the beginning of that story. And as Ignacio José Conti will learn, he will never truly be able to leave, or to return.

Batata's Flight

Don Manuel Rodríguez had a tin plates shop on América Avenue, in Villa Pueyrredón, a neighborhood right at the end of Argentina's capital, Buenos Aires, where the metropolis tried hard to keep the provincial life at a distance and the lower middle class tried hard to keep the uncomfortably close provincial poverty at a distance. The man used to make an infernal noise when he worked. This was a matter of necessity and tradition. The tradition of being noisy, however, was not followed only by practitioners of his trade. The noise from his shop was often lost in that of trolley cars, buses, carts, people congregating at the two pizza places on the block, and the customers standing in front of the market just three doors away from the tin plates place.

Don Manuel's son, Carlos, was going to a technical high school. He was interested in aviation, had made innumerable model airplanes, and had won various contests with them. Carlos had now embarked upon producing his master work: the moto-copter. This machine was something like a skyrocket/Model T Ford, or a motorcycle with wings. To say "airplane" or "helicopter" would be both to exaggerate and to fall short of the mark at the same time. The moto-copter seemed a tin spaceship wrinkled by the heat.

It was the conversation piece of the neighborhood. Carlos was building it behind the tin plates shop, where neighbors and clients often went to admire it. Even the police showed up once. They suspected that the plater was an anarchist involved in a conspiracy to overthrow the government, and that using his son's interest in aviation as a front, he was actually building a homemade tank to carry out his subversive purposes. As soon as the agents of law and order saw the machine, however, they silently departed, never to return.

One Saturday morning, at around 11:00, Carlos was giving the final touches to his moto-copter. The kerosene engine sounded like a choked lawn mower. One could clearly hear it from the street, where many folks were rushing by in order to end the workweek as soon as possible.

Attracted by the engine noise, a few passers-by had gathered in the back of the shop. They stood there, admiring the machine and waiting to see whether it would explode. Batata, a 12-year-old boy, whose big body was matched only by his limited lights, and who was crazy about birds and all sorts of flying things, stood there, too. His enthusiasm had no limit when he heard that the machine could fly. He had people repeat it to him various times. He wanted to know whether it flew like sparrows or like humming birds. And to reassure himself that the machine could fly, he turned to Carlos and his schoolmate Ignacio, and to whomever had the patience to answer him.

When least expected, Batata climbed up on the machine. Who knows what buttons he pushed. The truth is this: before anyone could stop it, the moto-copter ascended vertically, hesitated in the air for a moment, and went flying away over the market—maddening dogs, terrorizing birds, and giving the pet monkeys of the neighborhood a new occasion to scratch their heads.

An enormous cry arose from the street.

Batata, mounted on his machine, yelled more than anyone else, whether out of fear or joy is still unclear. In the middle of everyone, Batata's mother cried hysterically, shouting at him that he better come back or she would break his head.

The moto-copter and its rider continued shrinking into the distance, leaving the world of pedestrians and madmen, and entering that of the air force and the angels. The growing crowd hastily followed. The machine flew at very low altitude over the area, toward the Northeast. When it reached the outskirts of the city, it ran out of kerosene. It fell on a chicken coop after knocking down three billboards and a telephone pole.

As the pursuers arrived, they found that Batata had only a few bruises. His face, however, was transfigured. He talked without stopping—but one could only make out a single phrase: "The Virgin of Carmen." Upon hearing him say this, some old women began to make the sign of the cross. The rumor ran through the crowd—"Batata saw the Virgin." People shouted "Miracle!" They were entirely right. It was a miracle that the machine had flown. It was a miracle that Batata had not killed himself when he fell. It was a miracle that only one chicken had perished.

After a while, the police arrived and put the curious to flight. Batata's mother and Carlos' father were arrested because of the illegal actions of their children, and had to pay the fines established by law. Carlos was given an award at school, as the principal said, for having contributed to the progress of Argentine science with his flying machine. His father beat him up for the same reason.

Since that day, Batata has become the neighborhood's hero and saint. Soon afterwards, he was sent to a special school with money collected by the neighbors. He died from a stroke two years later. Eventually, some of the neighbors gathered signatures to ask for his canonization. But that never amounted to anything.

Carlos finished high school and then became the neighborhood mechanic. At the door of his shop, there is a plaque dedicated to Batata, the first human being to fly across Villa Pueyrredón in a moto-copter. Inside on a pedestal are the remains of the machine.

Margarita's Wedding

Margarita Vilar had not wanted to marry Arturo Monetta; but her mother, Lucía, was of a different opinion. Monetta had just inherited a house which his godfather had left him upon his death, and seemed to be hard working and in good health. This is all that mattered to Lucía, who had given signs of being a romantic when she was young, but had lost all traces of it after four years of helping her husband at a fish shop in downtown Buenos Aires, and decades of standing in front of the looms at the Cotton Company to support the four daughters her husband had left her as a gift when he had died from pneumonia during their fifth year of marriage. Margarita was old enough, and it was time for her to get a husband, and according to Lucía, Margarita's economic future had to be ensured by the wedding.

Overcome by maternal insistence, and seduced, like so many girls, by the promise of feeling (for one night) like Queen Isabella the Catholic or the Virgin Mary, walking toward the altar followed by floating celestial veils and the diaphanous train of the wedding gown she imagined, Margarita opted for security and pomp, and put love aside. The rest was in the hands of her mother, her sisters, and the family of the groom.

In the midst of the preparations for the wedding, two questions arose: "Where was the wedding to take place?" and "Where were bride and groom going to live once married?" The first question was resolved by both Lucía's poverty and the pride of the Monettas. The ceremony was not going to take place in the bride's home, despite tradition, as Lucía Vilar and her daughters rented the back of a clothing store in the modest to poor neighborhood of Villa Pueyrredón, and this was not the proper place for a wedding of the planned magnitude. Nor was it going to take place in a church, because this would diminish the ceremony by isolating the divine acts from the human party. The Monettas declared that it would be both their honor and happiness to have their son marry Margarita in the house the family had in San Martín, a small suburb of Buenos Aires where majestic country mansions intermingled with new land subdivisions ready to harbor the incipient Argentine middle class. Humiliated by her lack of means and happy to save herself the expense, Lucía Vilar accepted.

The other question—the one about where bride and groom were going to live once married—was more problematic. The obvious candidate was the house Arturo Monetta had just inherited, which also was in San Martín. It had been built on a corner lot, and was long and narrow with a small lawn in the front. It had a living room whose window opened to the lawn and whose doors opened one to the lawn and the other to the main dining room, which in turn was connected to the first of a series of bedrooms, a bathroom, and a kitchen—all connected with each other. As is the case with so many homes in this country, a gallery stretched alongside this house from the living room to the kitchen. Each room in the series had a door which opened to the gallery, and a little beyond, to a small narrow garden where tomatoes and hydrangeas grew.

The house was more than sufficient for the future newlyweds. The only difficulty was that it had not been used by the family since Arturo's godfather's death, and with a shortage of housing already affecting the area—increasingly inundated with both European immigrants and people from the interior, all fugitives from misery determined to survive and dreaming of a better life—some squatters had illegally settled in the place, and there was no way of getting them out by appealing to them directly.

The Monettas decided to defend their property rights without any weakness. According to the practices of the country, they got in touch with a friend of a friend who knew someone in the Police Department, to whom they were promptly introduced and to whom they described the situation, asking him to see whether he could do something about the matter, of course, without going to great lengths, assuring him that they were certainly going to keep it in mind, and giving him some eggs they had brought from their San Martín house and also, as they said, "something" for a cup of coffee. The man insisted that he did not take care of such things and that he would not accept anything for himself, but that he would determine if there were someone in his office who was disposed to do the job, and that he would for the moment keep the eggs and the rest because these things sometimes helped convince people.

The Monettas left, and on the next day, the friend of the friend of the acquaintance came down to their home to let them know that everything had been taken care of the night before; that it seemed there had been some resistance and some occupants had ended up injured; that the Monettas could get into the house where some of the windows' glass was broken; and that there still remained a few worthless things belonging to those who had been occupying it. The police, of course, had kept any valuable items in order to investigate. The family did not need to take any further action. The whole affair was entirely in the hands of the authorities.

Relieved by the news, Arturo's relatives, with the help of Lucía Vilar and all her daughters, except Margarita (because the bride was not supposed to take care of anything), began to get the house ready for the bride and groom. The wedding date had already been set, and as always in these cases, there was very little time left.

When the night dreamt of by Margarita and planned by the others arrived, Juancito, a cousin of hers, wearing formal attire, went to pick her up at the Villa Pueyrredón house in a luxurious vehicle—enormous, shiny and dark, like a carriage without horses—with the inside light on, so that people could see the bride on her nuptial trip. Her mother and sisters, with tears in their eyes for both aesthetico-psychological reasons, and out of tradition, accompanied her to the automobile, walking slowly and giving her last minute advice which the emotion did not let her hear. The neighbors had gathered, and also with tears in their eyes, saw her climb up slowly into the vehicle, sit upright and stiffly in the middle of the wide back seat, and smile to everyone and no one through the small window, which though appearing insignificant, separated reality from fantasy.

The limousine proceeded slowly toward the outskirts of the city, avoiding the ubiquitous potholes in the streets, awakening the curiosity of the people sitting at the doors of their homes, and exciting the shouting children who followed it every now and then. After crossing the railroad tracks which separated San Martín from the universe, they arrived at the town square, through which they were just supposed to pass, but around which the car began to go in slow and unending swings which Margarita, lost in her reveries, only noticed when a crowd of locals had gathered and was applauding her each time she passed. Terrified by the notoriety, and by the possibility of being late to the wedding, and sitting very stiffly so that no one would notice her nervousness, Margarita exclaimed, "Juancito! Juancito! What are you doing?! Take me to the wedding. I'm going to be late! Juancito! But Juancito! Come on cousin! I'm not in a joking mood!"

Juancito, as if nothing had happened, kept on driving around the square showing his cousin to the world, and to his cousin, no pity. Desperately in tears upon seeing her nuptial fantasy threatened by the reality of clocks and the growing impatience she could feel from a distance in the Monettas' home, she lost her composure, forgot her imaginary royal crown, and began to knock frantically on the sliding glass window that separated her from both the engine's noise and her cousin's caprice. He, as inexplicably as before, took a last solemn swing around the square and directed the car toward its original destination, free now from the circular spatio-temporal trap in which it seemed to have fallen, but not from the enthused crowd which now was following it as if beginning the party before the wedding. Margarita, calmer, prayed in the back seat to defend (without really recovering) her fantasy.

No one could ever explain Juancito's action. Some think it was an omen of things to come, but cannot specify what these things turned out to be. Others think Juancito was trying to tell Margarita that she should marry for love, not merely security. Still others, less kind, think Juancito was simply enjoying his temporary power. At any rate, these speculations are left to future gossip and biography. The important thing was to get on with the wedding.

When they arrived at the marriage house, everything was ready. The hired musicians were already playing the wedding march as some children had recognized the bride's car at a distance and announced their discovery with jumps and shouting. In the midst of the crowd gathered at the door, Lucía Vilar, who had also reached the place by car, but by way of a much more direct route, was waiting for her daughter to accompany her through the crowd toward the back of the house. There, the altar was ready, and there, awaited the groom and security, together with a bishop the Monetta family had asked to officiate at the ceremony.

With Margarita's mother were her niece and nephew, Rosita and Paquito Gómez, six and four years old respectively, who had been selected unanimously to hold the long veil train of the bridal gown when Margarita walked toward the altar. And so high were expectations, that for an instant, silence held dominion over all mouths when the car stopped in front of the house.

A child rushed to open the back door, hanging from the handle while the car dragged him during the last meter of its route. Margarita, again in heaven, stepped out and stood there, as if standing on those clouds on which she had once, when she was a small girl, seen the Virgin Mary. She extended her arm toward her mother, and both of them, solemnly and slowly turning—just like in the movies—began to walk through the crowd of relatives, friends, and others crashing the party, who barely opened up a path to let them pass. They were followed by Lucía's niece and nephew, delicately but firmly holding the veil train (per the directions they'd repeatedly been given) as if it were a small bird that they didn't want to let fly away.

When the four of them walked into the second room of the long Monetta mansion, one of Lucía's sisters, Calala Ruiz, could not restrain herself when she saw Paquito in formal attire and holding the veil train with the unreal seriousness of someone carrying out his first adult mission in life. "What a beauty!" she shouted as in a trance, and picked him up holding him tight and covering him with humid kisses full of rouge, which combined with the respiratory difficulty produced by Aunt Calala's hug, made tears come to his eyes. But a strong sense of duty helped him master his inexperience, and regaining his composure, he held the veil train tight so as not to let it go for anything in the world (per those directions). If an end of the train would give, it was not going to be his. Rosita waited next to him, bewildered, without knowing what to do or say.

Margarita and her mother, in the meantime, kept on walking slowly and solemnly together, both of them in the clouds of the Virgin but also nervously aware of a fact almost imperceptible to everyone else: the veil train, slowly, had stopped brushing the floor and had begun to stretch a little bit more at each new step taken by mother and daughter. It did not take many for Margarita to feel the pull in the ceremonial headdress, attached with hairpins to her locks. Grabbing on to her mother with one hand and holding on to her headdress with the other, Margarita stopped suddenly, and making a vain effort to maintain the solemnity proper to the moment, said in a slow but irritated voice: "Aunt, let the kid go. Let the kid go, aunt." Time seemed to have stopped. Aunt Calala, in ecstasy over Paquito's paradigmatic childhood beauty, would not let him go, and the child, absorbed in the strict fulfillment of his duty, would not let the train go. In the end, someone among those present freed the aunt from her aesthetic ecstasy, and so Paquito from his aunt's sticky embrace, and consequently Margarita from her momentary infernal eternity. Mother and daughter, again in the paradise of fantasy, resumed with their slow march toward the back of the house, the altar, the bishop with his blessing, and the groom with his security.

The rest was as they had dreamt it. The ceremony came to an appropriate end without further flaws, and the party went on until dawn—disturbing the sleep of dogs but not of humans, as the latter had all been invited (or had invited themselves) to the party. With its thousand or more people present, singing and dancing, the celebration had spilled out into the streets and the quiet country mansions of San Martín with carnivals of forgetfulness and hope.

At 1:00 a.m., bride and groom, more from fatigue than love, departed to spend their wedding night at Arturo's house. They then planned to visit the Atlantic coast for their honeymoon. When they arrived at the house, everything was perfect. They entered silently, walked hugging each other toward the bedroom determined to make that night's fantasy eternal, and then noticed the first few drops of the famous deluge of the 1930's. It rained, and rained, and rained during what was left of the night, and the rain reminded them of their good fortune as compared with that of those who had been forced from the house before another dawn not so long before. And lost in the reverie of love, they fell asleep while the waters rose.

The town of San Martín was ready to deal with torrential rains. The streets were quite deep—canals—with elevated sidewalks on top of their walls, connected on the street corners by small and very narrow revolving iron bridges which pedestrians had to turn in order to cross when the floods came. Bride and groom had nothing to fear.

At about 8:00 the next morning, Arturo and Margarita woke up, startled by a loud noise, resounding from the street. Bump! Bump! Bump! could be heard intermittently, ominously, as if someone had set out to dismantle the universe. They got up slowly, half asleep and confused, asking themselves what that might be, and went toward the front door, not quite dressed, to investigate. When they opened it, muffled cries filled their mouths. The water in the canals was as high as the sidewalks and covered the small iron bridge which crossed the street right in front of the house's door. Insistently bumping against it, some half open and letting their lugubrious cargo show, were coffins from the nearby cemetery, which because of the flood had floated up to the house. It was as if they were also searching for shelter and demanding the right to stay in the house Arturo had inherited from his godfather. Then, the new husband and wife began to understand the great limitations, real as well as fantastic, of the satisfaction and the security they had just obtained.

A Genuine Option

When Ignacio José Conti had just turned twenty years old, he fell hopelessly in love for the first time in his life. She, Amanda Mackenzie, was a beautiful brunette with green eyes, an easy smile, a slender body, and unlimited sex appeal. He met her on a Friday evening. Amanda was going to the theater with some of José's friends. He ran into them downtown. They were in a hurry. He talked with them for a few minutes, but they soon parted.

José was mad with love. For about two weeks after this encounter, he did nothing but remember Amanda, pronounce her name aloud, and fantasize innumerable scenes in which he told her he loved her. In them, she sometimes threw her arms around him and told him the most tender things imaginable. Other times, she was distant, and said they should wait, let time go by. And yet other times, she simply rejected him.

When he awakened from these daydreams, he realized it was too late to take his engineering finals. They would not be given again until the fall. This, however, did not disturb him in the least. His mind was somewhere else. With the absolute unavoidability of a 20-year-old's impulses, he determined to do the impossible and run any risk for that woman.

But did she love him?

How could he find out?

He needed evidence.

José phoned the friends with whom he had seen her, hoping to be invited to where he could see her again, or to hear some suggestive comment. It was largely in vain. Someone did give him her phone number, but no opening—nothing.

An entire week went by and his frustration became immense.

One of those Buenos Aires summer nights in which the bittersweet smell of the estuary excites every spirit, and the heat, the humidity, the crickets and the full moon conspire to keep the city's inhabitants awake, he decided not even to try to sleep. He liked to stay up when the city grew calm and the ancient silence from the pampas recovered its rights. And on a night like that, it was certainly better than the unavoidable alternative of nervously turning and turning, unendingly entangled in twisted and humid sheets.

He began to glance at a book he had found at the Lincoln Library, where he used to spend hours listening to jazz records. The book, forgotten on a chair, had attracted his curiosity and he had checked it out. It was *The Will To Believe*, by William James, about whom he knew nothing. Distractedly, he read:

> "Turn now from these wide questions of good to a certain class of questions of fact, questions concerning personal relations, states of mind between one man and another. Do you like me or not?—for example. Whether you do or not depends, in countless instances, on whether I meet you half way, am willing to assume that you must like me, and show you trust and expectation. The previous faith on my part in your liking's existence is in such cases what makes your liking come. But if I stand aloof, and refuse to budge an inch until I have objective evidence . . . ten to one your liking never comes. How many women's hearts are vanquished by the mere sanguine insistence of some man that they must

love him! He will not consent to the hypothesis that they cannot. The desire for a certain kind of truth here brings about that special truth's existence . . ."

He did not read any further. At once, he knew perfectly well what he was going to do.

He phoned Amanda the next day. He reminded her of who he was and told her that she loved him, and he loved her, and it made no sense for them not to be together forever. There was a long silence—as if Amanda was perplexed. He invited her to go out. After a moment of hesitation which felt to him like an eternity, who knows whether tempted by curiosity or vanity, she reluctantly accepted. They agreed he would pick her up shortly afterwards. José hung up, blessed James, crossed his fingers, got dressed, and left.

They had a drink at a downtown cocktail lounge. José did most of the talking, and again and again, told her that he loved her, she loved him, and they should stick together. Amanda was serious. She said nothing. Eventually they left the place, silently.

He was about to continue, but her sarcastic expression stopped him. Among the traffic noises and the downtown crowd, her farewell was curt and scornful: "If you quit putting on airs, you might at least be bearable. Good-bye. Thank you for everything, Rodolfo Valentino."

And he saw her walking away forever into the city's bustling streets, shattering his recently acquired faith in faith.

Frustration

It was his friend and fellow student at the Engineering School, Ricardo Morales, who told him "One has no right to know the world if one does not know one's own land." This touched José because he had always felt a certain intellectualized obligation to know his country and a certain equally intellectualized shame to know only Buenos Aires, the metropolis where he had spent his life until then, the early 1960's. Not to mention his presumptuous and naïve yearning for local color, his imprecise hostility toward his life in the big city, and his claustrophobic feelings concerning his urban surroundings; all of which reinforced his equally imprecise pastoral fantasies about grandfather Giuseppe, born among the goats and sheep of Abruzzi e Molise. (This fact could be found in the Italian language book of the Dante Alighieri Academy that José had attended to learn his family's original language.)

Hence, momentarily putting aside his escapist dreams of going abroad, but still driven by his pastoral romanticism and feelings of hostility—and claustrophobia—towards anything urban, José Conti decided to leave for the Argentine provinces. He would get to know them first hand. And furthermore, he would avoid taking trains or interstate buses, or going on those "camping trips in the solitude" promised by the postcards (and made certain by the occasional lack of transportation). Nor would he concern himself with the rumored guerrillas, or the consuetudinary and invariably unforeseen military exercises. So he set out to travel by local buses and to stay with the people of the towns along the way. He was not going to be a tourist. Not even a camera did he bring. And forget hotels! The more local the buses, the more removed the towns, and the closer the lodging to the lives of the people, the better.

There was, however, one gap in his itinerary. According to the information José had gathered in the cosmopolitan capital, no local buses could bring him from one northern province he'd be visiting, La Rioja, to another, Catamarca. Aware of how limited the details about the provinces tended to be in the big city, and also anxious to find adventure, he thought best to make inquiries about the local buses when he got there.

After half a month of visiting various parts of the country, José arrived in La Rioja's capital, his yearning for local color still intact, despite the fact that his money had diminished and his apprehension had increased. For he had lost his wallet (and almost his life) in a humiliating encounter with an inhospitable rattlesnake that had settled in a bag which he'd left on the shore of a lagoon during a swim.

Despite this disquieting experience, José continued without hesitation to the province's Tourism Bureau to find out about the transportation. The Bureau had only one employee—who sat behind an austere desk in an otherwise empty room in an old, but well kept building. José explained that he wanted to travel by local bus to Catamarca and stay in the small towns along the way.

The man responded, "Traveling by local buses is possible. It isn't comfortable, but one can do it. Finding room and board in the towns is quite another matter. In some, it may turn out to be impossible. Take Shaki, for example. This is the first town the bus goes through. Unless Doña Gonzalina is still alive, you won't find any room or board there. And I don't know whether the woman is still alive. Last time I saw her was about ten years ago. She was strong and active, still managing her farm and making ends meet with the little income she could get by offering lodging to people like you, who wanted to spend the night in the town. But then she was already 80 or 85. And I haven't heard from her since. She may have died."

José, filled with enthusiasm for adventure and metropolitan pride, unreflectively answered that he would run the risk. As if to justify his decision and hide his arrogance, he mentioned that it was summer, and though the mosquitoes might prove to be a nuisance, he was not going to freeze out there in the open.

The man mumbled something about ravenous mountain lions, laughed, and said, "It's up to you. Good luck. And if Doña Gonzalina is still alive, please, give her my regards. My name is Juan Otero." And he proceeded to tell José where to find the bus to Shaki.

José thanked him, said good-bye, and headed toward the bus stop, lugging his overly large and heavy suitcase. During the last two blocks of his long walk, he hardly had the strength to keep it from dragging, and felt embarrassed.

Upon arriving, he sat on the suitcase and waited for a couple of hours until the bus showed up far behind schedule. As soon as the driver got off the bus, José bought a ticket from him, climbed into the vehicle, and found a place for his bulky luggage in the front by the gear box (it wouldn't fit anywhere else). He sat nearby, where he thought he'd be able to see both the landscape and his property.

The vehicle gradually filled with much of the country—infants and elderly, pregnant women, bundles of all shapes and colors, and lots of cackling hens and roosters, held by their legs by their owners. José lost sight of his suitcase and soon began to feel claustrophobic. Everyone else seemed perfectly accustomed to traveling in such conditions. After half an hour of announcements, pushing and shoving, complaints, excuses, farewells, and last minute changes of seats (during which the driver fruitlessly tried to count and account for each passenger, animal and bundle), the bus groaned to a start. It crossed the town very slowly, finally leaving it behind, hesitating and bumping in a northwesterly direction on a long, hot, red-dirt road. Now it was mid-afternoon, and no trees were anywhere in sight.

Nothing moved except the bus and the distant dust devils that ran parallel to the mountain range and horizon, which alternately shrank and stretched toward the meager snow on the mountain peaks.

After traversing the desert for about five hours, the bus arrived in Shaki. The town, with its tall poplars and low intricate vineyards, suddenly emerged from behind a hill, offering an alternative to the prickly bushes which had been covering the dry red land. Shaki was very small—a few small farms on one side of the dirt road, and a bar on the other. The town got its water from a creek which ran behind the farms from somewhere up in the nearby mountains. It carried a fair amount of water when the snowcaps melted and only a trickle the rest of the year. There were just as many farms as the water could support—ten. And there were just as many bars as the need— constrained by the poverty of the locals could support—one. It was amazing the town was even on the map. Indeed, it was amazing it had a name.

José asked the driver whether he could be dropped off at Doña Gonzalina's place. He thought the man might not know her, but apparently the woman was known in the region and the driver stopped at the end of town. He pointed to an old house with mud walls that had been white, and with a straw roof that had attempted to withstand too many winds. José got out of the bus dragging his increasingly heavier and dustier suitcase, crossed the road, and walked slowly toward the house.

A young woman came out. He asked for Doña Gonzalina, and soon realized he was speaking to her granddaughter. The old woman then emerged, walking fast and addressed him in a loud, high-pitched voice, "Good evening, son. How can I help you? Have your lost your way—or your mind—to be in Shaki?" He smiled and mentioned Juan Otero, who had both sent his regards and directed him to her for room and board. The nonagenarian didn't seem to remember the man, but was happy to receive his regards and gain a customer. She led José into the house and asked him whether he liked goat. He had never tried it, but said that he did.

The granddaughter led him to his room, which was in a small building not far from the house. She opened the door and stepped aside to let him get in. He did so, dropped his suitcase on the room's stone floor, looked around curiously, briefly examined the mythological designs on the bedcover, and asked for the bathroom. She pointed past the vineyard's intricate maze of low-lying branches toward the unseen creek.

He looked, but could not see much. It was already getting dark and the twisted. entangled branches kept out any significant light. He began walking through the tangle toward the bathroom, his head and back bent forward to both avoid contact with the lowest branches as well as to see the shadowy ground underfoot. He had just taken a few steps when he lost his footing and began to fall. His body suddenly straightened up in an automatic attempt to avoid hitting the ground. His head smacked a branch instead. Confused and in pain, he turned to the woman, who was laughing. "Where's the ground around here?" he asked. She explained that the whole area under the vineyards was criss-crossed by irrigation ditches to make sure the water which came from the mountains quenched the thirst of the land as much as possible. She said that she'd get a kerosene lamp so he could find his way. José waited in the darkness, reassured only that he still had a body by the need to unload his burden. He could hear her laughter slowly receding.

When the woman came back, he took the lamp she had brought him and began crossing the vineyards very cautiously, lowering his head once again and feeling out with one foot at a time in order not to stumble and fall. He found the toilet on the other side of the vineyards. The three walls were no higher or wider than four feet each. The front was covered with a piece of canvas hanging from the side walls. Inside, there was a hole in the ground.

He hurriedly set the lamp in a corner, close to the hole. By then, he already felt an enormous need to relieve himself, and fully intended to do so. But in that stinking corner of the human desert there were a hundred thousand huge and hungry mosquitoes. José did not dare pull down his trousers. Overcoming his present discomfort with his fear of that of the future which those poisonous monsters threatened, he decided to wait until the next day. He simply urinated as fast as he could, using one hand to make sure his aim was as good as the circumstances permitted, and the other to keep the mosquitoes at a respectful distance from his tender and succulent skin. As soon as he finished, he quickly zipped up his trousers, picked up the lamp, and fled in a humiliating but prudent retreat toward the house. The mosquitoes stayed behind, irritated because of the visit. His underwear stayed with him, wet because of the rush. He had thoughts of leaving the town as soon as possible, but the bus passed by only every other day. He began to feel claustrophobic—this time in a rural, not urban environment.

Dinner was almost ready when he entered the house. A Chilean radio station was blaring rock-and-roll. Doña Gonzalina offered him some wine. He said he drank only water. Amazed and amused by his response, the woman said laughingly, "Son, not to drink wine in this province is a mortal sin. Are all Buenos Aires people water-wasters like you? No wonder we don't have any here. You people use it all up!" But then, becoming serious, she added, "Actually, not to drink wine is a good thing. Look at all the men around here! Have you seen any? Of course not! You haven't because they spend the whole day getting drunk at the bar. There would be no farms around here were it not for us, the women, who work rather than drink. These men are good for nothing. They only know how to spend on alcohol the money we women make. But are you sure you don't even want a small glass?"

José assured the woman that water was fine, and asked her whether there was any source of work other than the farms in the area. She laughed and said, "Why have another source of work if no one wants to work? The farms are work enough." He suggested that building a dam in the area might bring more water to the town, as well as people and jobs. And there had to be something worth mining in the nearby mountains which would help the town prosper, improving everyone's life and maybe in this way making alcohol less important to many.

Doña Gonzalina was greatly amused by these ideas. "But my son," she answered. "There's been talk of building a dam in the area since I was a young woman. And there's no dam around yet. Go look! See if you find one! Rattlesnakes! That's what you'll find." She chuckled and went on. "And why build a dam? If a dam were built, someone would take all the water for himself anyway. We're downstream, you know. We have to complain to our upstream neighbor every day to make him let the water come down to our farm. He closes the main canal locks, which are on his farm and then always forgets to reopen them. As a result, the water stays on his farm unless we force him to let it flow downstream. Do you think he'd remember if there were more water? He'd sell it out of town! This place is as close to paradise as it can get. I've heard talk of mining the mountains for at least as long as I've heard talk of building the dam. But nothing happens. Once in a while, someone comes with a few donkeys, puts a load of stones on their backs, and rides away with it. That gives no one here any work. And anyway, who wants it? The women around here already have enough. And the men want money, not work. And if by chance there happens to be money, they drink it. Things in Shaki are as good as they can get: we sing, pray, travel in our own way by listening to the Chilean radio stations, and once in a while have a big party. One can even make the best out of hell." Doña Gonzalina smiled thoughtfully.

José missed the sticky humidity he had always hated in Buenos Aires. The desert's dry silence had colonized the place.

Once dinner was over, he quietly mentioned he was going to his room and asked to be awakened around 7:00 the next morning. Doña Gonzalina, as if startled from a deep sleep, asked, "What for? Tomorrow is Sunday." He said he'd like to see the area. The woman laughed. "There's nothing to be seen around here. There are only hills, and the prickly bushes, and the stones in the creek back there. Even the ghosts have abandoned this *paramo*." José smiled and went to his room. Twisting whirlwinds of dust spun into his memory, while macabre dances of penitent souls began teasing his imagination. He fell asleep listening to the mosquitoes in the room, the shouting of the men in the bar across the road, and the hushed singing and praying of the women in the house.

He was awakened the next morning by a knock on the door and a woman's voice telling him it was 8:00. He arose, washed with the water from a small basin he'd found in his room and filled outside, and hurried toward the toilet by the creek, hoping to be able to relieve himself now that the mosquitoes should have left. He was right in thinking many had left. Many, however, had remained, and had been joined by thousands of ferocious horse flies in the sacrificial stall. Once again, he could only urinate while having to defend his skin and his virility. He felt sick to his stomach and went for a walk thinking that the bushes in the hills might be more hospitable for his physiological needs than Doña Gonzalina's facilities.

The creek bed was a chaos of dry stones and he began walking over them in an urgent search for a place to unload his painful burden. He had just begun to hide in some bushes, when he saw a man and a goat, both stern in appearance, ambling toward him with a distrustful gait. The man's determined right hand held a huge, shining machete. His left hand held a thick rope tied around the goat's neck. There was no one else around to be seen. The stranger walked toward José with an almost expressionless face. Two meters before reaching him, the man stopped and abruptly asked him who he was and what he was doing there. José explained that he was visiting town and just taking a walk to admire the area. The man smiled strangely and said, "I'd heard there was a visitor. But what's there to be seen around here? Is the government sending you?" He sounded angry. His hand grasped the machete more tightly, as if ready to strike. For a second, José almost believed that he, not the goat, was the weapon's target. He feared he might end up defecating right then and there, pants up and everything, in front of the stranger. He tried to compose himself, stupidly smiled at the goat, and stuttered that the hills were beautiful and worth seeing. The man shrugged his shoulders, showing no sympathy. The strange smile returned to his face, and without saying a word, he walked away with his goat.

Man and beast soon disappeared behind a slope. José could now see no one around, but felt observed and tense. The bushes suddenly seemed much more inhospitable than Doña Gonzalina's. Hopelessly convinced that the hills had eyes, he returned to the house, drank the cup of coffee that was ready for him, distractedly chatted with the women for a while, and overcome by a feverish torpor, returned to his room and took a nap plagued with nightmares until dinner time. He got up, barely touched the food, and went back to bed after vainly visiting the toilet once again. He fell asleep, sick and startled, a victim of real pain and fantastic forebodings.

The bus was supposed to go by the town on the next day at about 4:00 p.m. The women did not want him to leave because they believed that he might be bringing rain from Buenos Aires with him. Indeed, clouds could be seen on the horizon for the first time in months. José kindly excused himself from performing the suggested meteorological wonder and explained that given his trip's schedule, he could not wait. However, his attempt at justifying his departure on the basis of time and schedules to people who structured their lives on the basis of seasons (and eternity) failed to convince them. Yet, by 3:00, he was already sitting on his suitcase at the bus stop in front of the bar. He did not feel sick any more. His discomfort was gone, leaving him prey to an increasing numbness and claustrophobia. He was eager to continue his journey.

A tall, big-bellied man came out of the bar, stumbled toward him, and asked what he was doing. José said he was waiting for the bus. Upon hearing his accent, the man guessed, "From Buenos Aires, uh? I used to live there. Do you want proof? Hear this." And he proceeded to recite the streets of Buenos Aires, first from North to South, and then from East to West. Buenos Aires is a long and wide city, so when the bus arrived, the man had not quite finished.

José climbed up into the vehicle after giving the suitcase to the driver, bought a ticket, and sat down in the first free seat he could find. Some of the passengers talked to him; but he could not answer. He again had just one thought—to find a bathroom in the next town.

Finally, having traversed the ubiquitous *paramo* of red land, dust, whirlwinds, and prickly bushes—for three hours—the bus reached Famatina, which was a bit larger than Shaki. It had twenty farms and two bars. Each bar had a boarding house in the back. He walked into one of them bearing his unbearable baggage. As soon as he reached the counter, an explosion was heard outside. The man behind the counter began to laugh like mad. The customers echoed him.

In the midst of the racket and still laughing, the man looked at José and cried, "Guess what that is!"

"An explosion," answered José, who did not know what to think of the matter.

"Yes. But what sort of explosion?" quizzed the man.

"I don't know. What is it? A bomb?" He had just asked this, when another explosion was heard and the laughter grew even louder, taking over the place.

"Warm," said the man trying to control his laughter. "But who causes the explosions?"

José was at a loss to guess. He thought of saying, "the guerrillas," but did not want to get himself into trouble.

The man continued, "It's the priest!"

"The priest?" asked José, perplexed.

"Yes," said the man. "He got tired of ringing the bells to call people to church and having no one show up. They always told him they hadn't heard them. You know, the hills are high and the valleys large . . . He's got them now! He gave up on the bell, got a cannon, and whenever he calls people to church, he fires it three times. There it goes for the third time! No one can lie to him any more. It can be heard throughout the region." The man started laughing again.

José laughed, too, and his laughter caused him pains that reminded him he absolutely needed a bathroom, and fast. He asked for it and for a room to stay.

A tall, heavy-set man in his fifties led him to his bedroom and pointed to the bathroom, which was next to it. José walked into his room, dropped his suitcase with approval, entered the bathroom, shut the door, and glanced toward the toilet. It was not a mere hole on the ground, but it was unusual, and made out of something like dried mud. Its walls were at most one inch thick from the base to the top (where ordinary mortals would normally sit). But the top edge was not flat as one would expect. It was covered with cutting edges, like circular saw teeth, pointing up all around. It must have been constructed to prevent contagious diseases from spreading: no human being could, without being a masochist, seriously consider the idea of sitting on it. He adopted the position closest to sitting that he could manage without touching the saw-like teeth, and stayed in this position for as long as he had to, which after three days of postponements, was quite awhile.

Finally, his physiological needs were satisfied. He felt cold and sweaty, and his muscles were tense because of the double effort— both gymnastic and physiological—he had made. Feeling relieved, he glanced around for toilet paper. There was none. Instead, the establishment had provided used primary school notebooks covered with colorful additions such as pictures of Donald Duck. This had to make do, and it did. But when José pulled the chain which hung from a small water tank above the toilet, nothing happened. He pulled again. Nothing.

Trying to hide his humiliation, he got dressed as soon as he could, stepped outside, approached the man who had guided him to his room, and said, "Excuse me. There's no water in the toilet tank."

The man looked at him as if enraged. "And what do you want with these governments?" he shouted. "Of course there's no water in the tank! There's no water coming from the kitchen faucets, either! Five years! It's been five years since we installed the plumbing in the entire house because those dirty politicians promised us running water! Have you seen the water? No! Nor have we! Because they took the water and rerouted it to the area where they had land. Of course, there's no water in the tank! If you want water, you have to take that bucket on the ground, go to the well down there, get water in the bucket, carry it back to the bathroom, and dump it in the toilet. That's the way life is around here."

Silenced by this reply that reminded him of a few others he'd heard in Shaki, and embarrassed by his naive urban assumption that if there is a water tank above the toilet, water should be expected to be in it, José picked up the bucket and went to the well. After hauling up some water, he carried it to the bathroom and dumped it in the toilet. A sick expression rose to his face—the drain was clogged. He now had to go back for help again, and who knows what political problem this might create, and what the reaction might be.

He walked slowly toward the same man, and once he was close enough to be heard, sheepishly said, "Excuse me, again. Do you have anything I could use to unclog the toilet? I believe it's clogged. In fact, I'm sure it's clogged."

The man looked at him with satisfaction. After a few seconds, he said, "Okay. Don't worry. I'll tell some of the kids in the house to take care of it."

José went and sat on a bench against the wall in the hallway, near the entrance to his room. He would have preferred to hide *in* the room; but it was being cleaned. It took almost half an hour for it to be readied. During this time, a couple of teenagers kept going in and out of the bathroom. Each time they came out, they stared at him, both in amazement and hate. He wished the ground would swallow him up. As soon as the room was ready, he went in and retired, passing up dinner out of sheer embarrassment. He was unable to sleep until very late. Red dust, whirlwinds, Donald Duck's smiling face, the full moon watching the life of mortals from the bottom of the well, and images of long and thick gray tears gushing out of the adobe walls swirled around his head. He finally fell asleep listening to a group of Indians as they sang Christmas carols in Quetchua. It was Christmas Eve and they had come to visit the nativity set up by the owners of the boarding house.

The next day, he left town. He sat very quietly in his bus seat and watched the dry world of desert towns and thwarted hopes remain unperturbed despite him. The local people had to carry a heavy load. His metropolitan world of options and development seemed more welcoming and less disgusting than when he had left it. Yet, something unsettling remained. The desert had become a part of everything.

The Wild Bull

No, man! I was upset but not about to start a brawl. The head, cool. It was the old man who exploded. It seems that during one of those nights when he stayed up pacing back and forth because an associate was playing it dirty, he thought, "This just can't go on any longer! If I die, the ticks will eat all of you!" Since I was the only son, and an adult, he presented me with an ultimatum the next day. He had me sit down in the living room with the old lady present and read the list to me. I wasn't going to spend my time anymore belly up pretending to be a poet or who knows what, because poetry without bread wasn't worth a dime—not devoting myself to anything useful was just wasting everyone's time and money—beginning one thousand studies without finishing any, from Quetchua, which who-on-earth cared about, to the artists' French, to the German that was going to be of use to me only if I went on with my engineering studies—instead of strolling through Francia Square or raving about topology or philology, or what is worse, putting on musician's airs and bringing home those two old pieces of junk—those church organs I was planning to reassemble in the small room out on the terrace which was never going to work out because I never finished anything—and if they ever worked, the house was going to collapse or the police were going to kick us out of the neighborhood and we were going to lose the house which had cost him a life of effort to buy so that the old lady, my sister and I could be well. That I'd do better to get a job with Uncle Leo, who was crazy but at least knew how to make millions and not to screw around like me—or that the old man would give me a little Fiat if I became an insurance agent— and if not, I should go work with him in his construction company and study civil engineering, or maybe law if I didn't like engineering anymore—that this was going to work out and we could start a realty company and everything was thought out with my sister an architect— and everything. But not vagrancy.

I, as you can imagine . . .

"Hey, waiter, bring me another cup of coffee!"

Like I said. I, as you can imagine, was irate. After all, I'm his son, man. I jumped up and called him on his tirade. And I told him that no one talked to me like that—that he should mind his own business—that freedom and the meaning of life are first—that what he lacked was cultural appreciation—that I thanked him very much for having given me an education—but that I was not about to sell myself—and that books were culture not a life investment. He could keep the corrupting little Fiat to himself. And what was wrong with those organs? After all, people had not understood Leonardo da Vinci, either. And if the house went to pot, so be it. It was full of ghosts and humidity and a cold that ate your bones and air currents and more rooms than a hotel downtown while some people were without a roof. One had to quit hiding behind middle-class ideology. Humanity was never going to be saved from the mediocrity of liberal ideas. I told him, "Greatness is extremist." And I split, and here you have me, a hired hand in the venerable Lisandro de la Torre Slaughterhouse, Mataderos neighborhood, wearing a white tunic but not that of physicians or of primary school kids, pushing carcasses, carrying barrels full of lukewarm brains or kidneys while I try to avoid slipping on the bloody sawdust on the ground (so no one around here loses respect for me), reading Spinoza and jotting down aphorisms while I take a stroll around the hanging carcasses in my free time, and living in the back of the milk shop which used to belong to the legendary Ramón Reyes until he lost it in the horse races and ended up as a cook at my family's house.

And I don't complain.

I know, I know. Things are bad. And the government of the unnamables has already made it plain—like Franco's Spain for about twenty years until we all walk straight like a German platoon. Of course, the money is nowhere to be seen and that which you do see, shrinks. But I'm closer to the workers. And as a student, I have a mission to fulfill—to unite the classrooms with the factories in the fight against imperialist aggression—and the ugly thing that's threatening us from within—when anyone you ask, from right, center or left, tells you the solution is violence. One has to learn from this morning's bull. Wild, man. Wild and no sell out. And what did they say? It only occurred to them to talk about waste, disorganization, sausages, and what not. The bull, man, had courage. They stuck it into the death walk, but at the end, the big guy with the eyes red from wine and the veins thick from blood was waiting to give it the *coup de grâce*, and where the bull was met by the shouting of agony and the smell of blood and entrails from the fourth floor. But *that* bull, no way. It was not about to take another step. It was going to die free and not let anyone turn it into hamburger. It jumped, committing suicide, and making a mess of the Peugeot owned by one of the *gringos* who own this bloody firm—which squeezes out our juice and our will to live. Yeah, of course, it didn't accomplish anything. But what alternative did the poor beast have? The knives of the fourth floor? Besides, it's the principle that counts. How do I know which principle? The principle! Give me a chance, brother! I haven't stopped learning yet, even though I may have lost my respect for our institutions of higher learning. True—one must act effectively. But how can you do it here with the general without a name putting a hole in the head of everyone who thinks? I don't know, man, I don't know. Try whatever we try, we're at a dead end. We're what they call "the lost generation." Maybe one can do something from abroad, but from within, forget it. I'm going to split. I'm not going back to work today. My message for the supervisor is that the "poet of the hanging carcasses" is leaving soon for a foreign country.

"Hey, waiter, come get your money!"

Like I'm telling you. I'm so down that, for freedom, I'd even take a plane to the great democracy of the North. No. I don't know Russian, man. And besides, they say that if you don't do well over there, you end up as cannon fodder in Vietnam. I'm not anyone else's casual hero. Neither Western, nor Christian, nor imperialist, nor capitalist, nor communist, nor Peronist. I am one with the universe. I know. There's also Italy—or the sister republics—but for that I'll stay here. And France—mother of liberty, won't get out of Africa, nor do the scholarships they give you provide enough to eat and you starve or try to get your lunch from the Seine. I'm fed up, man. I'm up to here with politics and causes. I'm merely a pawn for the powers that be. Maybe, if I go away and do some serious studying in the USA where foreign students don't starve—I'll be able to help from abroad some years down the road. I'll be like Ramón Reyes, but with better prospects and without a gambling habit! It's such a lonely prospect, though—I know I have friends—but life separates you from them. You, for one, are staying here. What's always there for you, if you're lucky to have it, is your family. No! I don't mean simply your biological parents—I mean your family— those who looked after you when you grew up, and those who grew up with you and came to care for you. I'm going to go see the old lady and the old man, who'll suffer when I disappear. It's been too long since I last saw them. And they love me. How could I have been so blind and ungrateful? How could I treated them so badly when I love them so much? I have to start all over with my life.

RETURNS

Isabel

After about a year of logic and smog in California, of freedom of expression, of freaks and hippies and French fries with ketchup, Ignacio José Conti returned to Buenos Aires for a visit, where he stayed with his parents in the Almagro neighborhood. One morning, he got up to find himself alone in the house. It was about 9:00, and there usually was someone around at that time. Half asleep and puzzled, he entered the kitchen to heat up some coffee. On the kitchen table, he found a brief note written by his mother: "Isabel tried to commit suicide. We have taken her to the hospital."

Isabel was the maid. She was fifteen years old. Her face was dark and alive, her body strong and slender. Both the fury and serenity of the jungle seemed to run through her body. She had lived on a farm in the northeast with her guardian until a year earlier, when he had thrown her out. Isabel had come to Buenos Aires to stay with an aunt who'd got her the job working as a maid. She had returned to school, and was doing well in the fourth grade. And she was lacking neither plans for the future, nor friends, nor the want of having a good time. In fact, Isabel went to every party she could. She often said that she was very happy living with the Contis. Then why suicide?

His mother came back after awhile and related what she knew. "This morning, I overslept. I got up at 8:00, and Isabel was still in bed. I thought this strange, because she's always up by then. So I went to see whether she was feeling all right. I knocked on her door, and she didn't answer. I knocked again, and she sighed, sounding like a sick little bird. I asked her whether she was all right, and she answered, 'I don't feel well.' I asked her whether she wanted me to bring her a cup of tea, and she said 'No. I poisoned myself, madam.' I almost died! I opened the door and cried, 'Child! Are you crazy? What did you do?'

"She had taken two tablespoons full of insecticide. Your sister and I rushed her to the hospital, but we don't know whether she'll live or not. The doctor says we won't know for a couple of days, because the insecticide she took won't take full effect right away. It attacks the liver after quite a few hours . . . What a disaster! And what am I going to tell her aunt? Isabel is a minor . . ."

José tried to calm down his mother as best as he could, but he didn't know what to say. They were talking when his girlfriend arrived. Carolina had been very close to Isabel. They informed her of what had happened, and she decided they should go to the hospital immediately. Meanwhile, his mother would have the grim task of giving Isabel's aunt the news.

When they arrived, the nurse on duty told them they could not see the girl. She also said that Isabel had received a letter from a certain Emilio before her suicide attempt. She had brought the letter to the hospital. The nurse showed it to them. It read:

Dear Isabel:

I never mentioned Leonor to you. I now ought to do so. Leonor and I lived together for ten years. Care, mutual respect, trust, understanding, and a strong sexual attraction kept us together during all that time. Together, we developed. Together, we shared the beautiful things and the difficulties of everyday life. We were always the perfect match for each other. Or, rather, we seemed to be so. One sad day, Leonor left me. She moved in with a man I believed to be my best friend. My solitude was unspeakable; my anguish, unbearable. But I am not writing to pity myself. I am writing because I have not overcome this tragedy yet. In fact, I cannot. Let me explain. When Leonor left, I did not actually lose anything. For Leonor and I did not really love each other We couldn't have, because what there was between us is over. And true love is indestructible. But what I now call 'love' can end—can be destroyed. So it cannot be love. Isabel, I am writing because I do not love you and ought to tell you so. Love does not exist. Nor can it exist. We are condemned to a solitude of hate and indifference. I, for one, cannot bear it. Only one course of action is left for me. Tonight. Tonight, everything will be over. Good bye, Isabel. Do not be sad, because you do not really love me either. Good bye.

— Emilio

Carolina and José returned home with more questions than before, and without any answers. When they arrived, Ramón, an old Spaniard who lived with the family, was standing at the door. He asked them about Isabel's health. They told him what they knew.

When they mentioned Emilio's letter, Ramón said, "Oh, yes! Some men from Channel 9 brought it yesterday while Isabel was watching television. I received the letter, gave it to Isabel, left for the dairy, and forgot about the whole thing"

Out of curiosity, José phoned Channel 9 and asked for Emilio.

The answer was curt. "Emilio committed suicide last night."

José wanted to know more, but whoever answered hung up. Before he had a chance to call again, Ramón walked in with a newspaper he had just bought. He showed it to them. The front page headline announced: EMILIO OSTADT COMMITS SUICIDE DURING BROADCAST. An account of the event followed:

Last night, when his soap opera series *María Rosa* was scheduled to end, the popular actor Emilio Odstadt committed suicide in front of the Channel 9 television cameras. After announcing that the time to part had come, and that all his admirers had received good-bye letters from him, Ostadt took a revolver out of his jacket, said 'Love does not exist,' and shot himself in the head. He died instantly.

They all sat down, and no one spoke for a long while.

After a few days, Isabel was discharged from the hospital. She said she was very happy to be alive. Everyone present laughed and no one ever mentioned the matter any more. Soon afterwards, José left again for the United States, never to see Isabel again. He later heard that she had finished high school and was working in a factory that manufactured nylon stockings.

The Museums

When Conti first left for the USA, the idea that he might stay there for more than two years did not even cross his mind. He had very definite plans to return and felt he was in control of his destiny. Back in his native Argentina in 1978, he had already spent more than a decade in the States and had not visited his country for about seven years. He still felt in control of his destiny, and his plans were as definite as they had always been, though different: to obtain a U.S. immigrant visa (the coveted green card which today is actually white).

His change in plans and his long absence from his country no doubt had rational explanations, but these resulted from those combinations of events which give shape to the lives of people regardless of their intentions. He had not returned earlier because he had lacked the money to go, or the visa to return; or he had sometimes been dissuaded from going by news of the turmoil in Argentina—or worried the American bureaucracies would turn his visit into a nightmare—or he had been enthralled by the love of a new girlfriend whom he just could not abandon in the middle of summer. Finances, caution, and love had conspired to keep José away from his land and his family.

The combination of circumstances and weaknesses which had kept him away for years eventually led him to realize that he was now resettled—for he already had work, friends, and a new life in the States. And it was this realization that enabled him to finally make the decision to return to his homeland. (And, of course, he wanted to apply for that permanent residency visa for his new country.)

Given this decision, the inexplicable Argentinian habit (or is it an obligation) of missing both one's country and dear ones to the point of utter depression when one is away (which remarkably changes when one returns to Argentina) did the rest. For though he had to leave to apply for his immigrant visa, he could have gone to Canada or Mexico, both more convenient to visit and less dangerous than Argentina for an opponent of the military dictatorship, particularly one like him, who had lost the habit of keeping his ideas to himself. And as his girlfriend sweetly and honestly reminded him (before the fight that ensued), it *was* less expensive, and she would be happy to go with him anywhere, even if it were not romantic like Quebec or Acapulco, but where he could end up tortured or dead. José was obstinate, desperate to reattach the severed umbilical, overcome by memories, and worried by the lack of news from his family. One love overcame the other, and the fear of the black Ford Falcons used by the Argentine police faded away.

So it is that he departed, as eager to walk the streets of Buenos Aires as to see his family—and eager to take a table at a timeless bar or café—to savor, slowly, a cup of something, while reflecting alone, about the nature of time and eternity, or with others, about the government's economic policies or the national soccer team. He had grown up in that city and loved it.

The visit began well. It was good to see his parents happy, his godmother healthy, his niece and nephew whom he had never seen, his sister and her husband busy with the kids, and these youngsters busy messing things up. It was also good to visit with the few of his friends who had not left the country. And of course, the city was still captivating. But it seemed more subdued than before, as if its inhabitants were simply waiting. In the old cosmopolitan Buenos Aires, this was either a sign of extremely hot weather or something wrong. And it was not too hot, not even for him, who during the preceding years had become accustomed to the incomprehensible cold of the North American Snow Belt.

José could not bring himself to believe how dramatically the city had come to a stop. To satisfy his curiosity, as much as to hold on to his memories, he set out to find out whether things had really changed to such an extreme. To begin with, he decided to visit the art museums. He phoned a few of them to ask when they were open, and to his surprise, was told they weren't. In some cases, no one answered. In others, those who answered told him that they had closed down for a couple of months. In the Buenos Aires that he remembered, this was impossible. In the Buenos Aires of his present, something sinister seemed to be at work behind the scenes.

Seeking a lost familiarity, he visited his sister and informed her of his calls to the museums. She thought the situation was as odd as he did, and left to look for a newspaper, where they could determine the museum schedules. José waited, with more confidence in himself and less in the city. After a short while, his sister returned, beaming with satisfaction and relief. The newspaper listed a number of museums he had not phoned, and the times at which they were open. He could go that very afternoon, and decided to do so.

He took the subway for the Museum of Modern Art, which opened for the afternoon at 3:00. Hypnotized by the rhythmic jerking of the noisy (and nearly empty) cars, his mind drifted back to the museum visits of his primary school days. The devoted teachers would lovingly, yet solemnly, guide the class through the surprises of modern art, the marvels of natural history, and the moral sagas of the Argentinian past. The slaves had been freed because they were human; General San Martín had relinquished power and left the independence armies in Simón Bolívar's hands rather than let South America's freedom be threatened; and President Mitre had refused to partition defeated Paraguay as victory gave no rights.

When the train reached his station, José disembarked, climbed up the stairs that ended on the street, and in the sweet expectation of recovering his long-treasured past, walked toward the museum. The street was noisy, but in his daydreams, all was quiet. He soon arrived at the museum and pushed through the main entrance door. Right behind it, two soldiers aimed their machine guns at him.

"You can't come in," one said. "This building is under military control."

"I want to go into this museum," replied José, perplexed. "The newspaper says it's open."

"We don't know about that," the other answered. "All we know is that the building is under military control—for an indefinite period of time—and that you can't come in."

Accustomed to the Buenos Aires he loved and remembered—and to that decade of freedom of expression in the North, José persisted. "Then how come the paper says the museum is open?" he demanded.

"We don't know," was the brusque response. They gripped their machine guns tighter. "Why don't you go to the back of the building? Maybe they'll let you in back there," one soldier suggested rudely.

As he knew very well, they were sending him to the city theater, which was housed in another wing of the same building. He said so, but headed there anyway as he did not seem likely to pass in through the main entrance. Recollections of a few foreign news reports in the USA led to growing uneasiness that was affecting his confidence and forcing his cherished memories further into the past.

As soon as he walked through the back door, he saw several men sitting around an empty table. They looked like policemen in civilian clothes. A number of them spoke to him at the same time.

"You can't come in. The building is closed."

"But I'm going to the museum," he answered hopefully.

"It's closed," came the fierce reply. "Besides, this is *not* the museum. This is the theater."

"But the newspaper says . . .".

"That's impossible," the man interrupted, without even looking at the paper José was opening.

"You'd better leave," another warned.

He left, angry and puzzled. Outside, the loudspeakers lining Corrientes Avenue were—by presenting military marches—preparing the people for both the World Cup (which was to be held in Buenos Aires) and for war with Chile over a border dispute in the Andes.

José tried visiting the other museums listed in the newspaper, but they were all closed. He returned to his sister's home, related the story of his aborted visits, and then became involved in playing with his niece and his nephew. He gave up on viewing art in the museums in Buenos Aires during his visit.

A few months after his return to the USA, he received a newsletter published by an international organization. The issue was devoted to political oppression in Argentina. It estimated the number of political prisoners at the time, and mentioned that many were incarcerated and tortured in museums. Then he heard hopeless cries of pain and horror, echoed by marble walls and works of art, together with his teachers' voices, indistinct but firm, teaching about art, nature, and the moral lessons of history.

The Passports

I know I just arrived, but you know how slow and irrational the bureaucracy is. Remember when, by law, I had to shave my beard to get my passport renewed, because the government argued that otherwise, terrorists could leave the country in disguise? And remember when I almost failed to return to the United States on time, because it took half a month to renew my passport? I won't get burned again. This time, I'm going to do what everyone does: find a friend and get the passport renewed in December, long before my mid-January trip. I'm supposed to begin teaching my classes here later that month, and want no complications. What do you mean friends are no help? They are the only thing that ever made Argentina work! I know— times have changed. No one knows a friend from an enemy after the "dirty war," and I have been away for too many years. My contacts are gone. So what do you propose? What? Now, that's a revolutionary idea! Going through the legal channels? Trusting the bureaucracy? Giving the system a chance? Obviously, Carolina, you've also been away for a long time and have lost touch. I know that the military are flat on their backs after last year's war with Great Britain, but the paramilitary machine is still intact. Besides, why trust that the legal channels will work at all? Is this the Argentine miracle? I see—it's not a matter of trust, but of desperation. We've lost our contacts and don't know who's a friend any longer. It makes me mad! This is what the oppression has done to all of us: trust and friendship can no longer flourish. Look at our families! The only friends they have are those they had before it all began. Besides, why on Earth does Argentina send its citizens to the Police Department to renew their passports? Why not do it like here, where people can go to the post office to renew them? I guess that battle was lost early in the century, when the national identification card became part of the life of each and every Argentine. You see? The dice had already been rolled. It was inevitable that we would become a military state. I don't know what I'm going to do. I guess I'll give the bureaucracy a try. I'll let you know how it goes—if I live to tell the tale.

Irma. Could you please call the travel agency and make a reservation for my trip to Spain? Yes, for two weeks from now. I told Calderón that I'd be in Madrid by January 15th to sign the papers, and want to make sure everything is in order. That's right. This contract is a big break for our company. In fact, with the economy as it is, we need it to survive. I don't want to lose it simply because I can't travel. By the way, could you please call Miss Beruti? Yes. You should have her phone number. She's the woman who had my passport renewed last time. It was processed as a diplomatic passport. That way, it takes only five days and I'll have my passport for sure. Otherwise, who knows what might happen? Here. Take my passport and tell her that Gustavo Pereira would like her to pick it up tomorrow. If she can't, ask her to please come the day after tomorrow. I don't want to delay the process much longer. Yes, you can go home after talking to her. I'll take care of closing the office.

I can't stand this life of waiting and wishing and fearing that they killed them. My son! My little Carlitos! My eyes, heart, and hope . . . Where have they taken you? All I know is you left the house to take an exam at the engineering school and never came back. And my dear Juan, my husband . . . What have they done to you? It was dark when they knocked at the door. I looked out, and could see five or six men in front of two black Ford Falcons . . . the headlights blinded me. I didn't want to open the door; but they threatened to smash it in. Then, it was all pain . . . they rushed in with their automatic weapons aimed at us. They kept on asking, "Where is it? Where is it?" Juan told them we didn't know anything about anything; but they didn't listen. They took the maid, poor soul, into the kitchen and interrogated her. We were forced to lie down facing the living room floor. For hours, there was all this noise of walking, opening drawers, and emptying closets throughout the house. Juan raised his head to see what was happening, and a boot heel pushed it down to the floor. I was crying. They hit me and told me to shut up. Then they forced Juan to go with them. I begged them to leave him alone, ran to the door behind them, and saw how they pushed him into the back of one of the cars. He never came back . . . Now I, the same Adelina Paz who would never get involved in politics, march in May Square with both of their pictures, together with all the other mothers, with their sorrow, and the pictures of their disappeared husbands, daughters, sons . . . It's exhausting . . . But I still do it, even though people call me crazy and some of my neighbors avoid me . . . I'm tired . . . consumed . . . I'm afraid I'm going to fail my family . . . Perhaps if I made a trip abroad, I could gather some support and get my energy back . . . Maybe those French women who visited with our group last month might be able to help . . . Yes . . . Of course . . . That's what I'll do . . . I'll take the fight abroad. I have to tell Cecilia and the others about it. What else do I need? The clothes I have will have to do. My suitcase is fine. I'll make an airplane reservation today. And I need to get a passport . . . Adelina Paz is no longer just a middle class housewife who never traveled abroad. She's a woman set on recovering her family. Just wait for me, Carlitos . . . Don't worry my dear Juan . . . I know what to do.

What a line! It has already taken an hour and I could only fill out the form. I hope Carolina is right and this works. Yes, I would like to have my passport renewed, sir. This is my passport and here is the form. How much is it? Why is it so much? When I have it renewed at the consulate in Chicago they charge me only 20% of that amount! Of course I want my passport, but why the difference in price? Why discriminate against Argentines who are in Argentina? OK—here's the money. Could you please tell me when the passport will be ready? Thank you. Next week will be fine.

Miss Beruti! What a pleasure to see you again! Would you like a cup of coffee? Nothing? Okay. Please sit down. As my secretary told you, I need a favor from you. This is my passport. I need to have it renewed, and as you know, one can't always trust the bureaucracy. Of course, as always, you can be sure I'll be eternally grateful to you. And if you will allow me, I would like to show my gratitude now. I hope $300 is sufficient to cover all your expenses and show my appreciation as well. Oh, you're very welcome. Five days? That will be fine. Where should I pick up the passport? At the Palace of Government? But that's an unusual place. Why not, as before, at the Police Department? I see. Where exactly? Through the main entrance and ask the man at the end of the corridor on the left. Very good. Thank you, and please give my regards to your mother. See you soon.

Yes, I would like to get a passport, please. This is my form and here is the money . . . I'm sorry . . . I thought I'd written my name clearly. It's Adelina Paz. Yes, Adelina Paz. Here is my national identification card. What am I supposed to do now? That line? Okay . . . And when can I come back to pick it up? I thought it took longer . . . I'll be here next week. Thank you very much.

Let me tell you, Carolina. These people have no manners. And they're not reliable at all. They told me the passport would be ready this week. I've already gone twice and it's always the same story: they don't have it. Tomorrow, I'm going back again—but not to that little window where everyone crowds up for passports. A friend of my sister knows someone who knows someone else who suggested that I ask for Captain Mazzi. I just hope he exists. If not, I'm caught in the bureaucratic maze I feared. I'll keep you posted—if I ever return from the Police Department.

What did she say? That I should not go to the Palace of Government, but pick up the passport at the Police Department on January 14th? But I travel on the 15th! Did she give you any explanation? I don't like this, Irma. Please call her back and ask her for a contact at the Police Department. Who should I talk to? Going blind to those places is just hopeless.

But this is the third time I've come here! What are they waiting for? Is there anyone I can talk to? I need to travel. I know that . . . so does everyone . . . but I've filled in all the forms. Why the delay? I have to see some people in France. Who? Mr. Portes . . . on the second floor? Thank you very much.

So what do you suggest, Captain Mazzi? I've gone, as you advised, to the Blue Room. Someone cracked open the door, asked for my name, and when I told him, said they were expecting no Conti there. I went downstairs to the central room, and you know very well what I found. Hundreds of passports were piled up on a multitude of tables in no discernable order. Some had fallen to the floor and a custodian was sweeping the passports into boxes that he pushed under the tables. I can ask someone for help, as you suggest—but who? There are about a hundred people walking around in that room. Those who are employees are rushing through the place and never answer any questions. The others are people like me, who are trying to find their passport among those scattered around the room. If, as you say, the police downstairs are "running a scam," then why aren't they stopped? Is there anyone else I could talk to? Okay—I'll try Mr. García, though going to the main counter didn't help before.

Do you know who I am? I'm Gustavo Pereira, of Pereira Manufacturing Ltd. I'm here to pick up my passport, which was brought to you for renewal by diplomatic courier. I know that's unusual. Yet, this is what Miss Beruti told me. I can't come back tomorrow. If I don't have it today, I'll lose a $10 million manufacturing contract that I'm supposed to sign in Madrid tomorrow. I'll go broke! Where should I look? In the central room? Okay. Here, this is for you. Get yourself a cup of coffee. If I can't find my passport, I'll be back for more help. What's your name? Okay, Mr. Molinari, I'll ask for you.

But Mr. Portes, I've seen the central room and can't imagine how I can find my passport there. It's crazy . . . They're lying on the floor under the tables, and people are pushing them around in desperation to find their own. A woman told me that 7,000 people are in this situation. Yes . . . My name is Adelina Paz. Will you please ask? Maybe, if you're correct, my passport is in the Blue Room. I'll wait here . . . Sorry? That I should go to the Blue Room? Thank you. I will.

Are you Mr. García? My name is Ignacio José Conti. Captain Mazzi told me that I should talk to you about my passport. It should be here. I've looked in the central room, but as you know, it's practically impossible to find anything there. Could you—perhaps—help me look? I'll certainly be very grateful—and by the way, this is for you. I know you're not asking for anything, but please take it as a token of appreciation from a friend. And thank you for coming with me to the central room. Can you see the chaos I was talking about? Why is this happening? The military upstairs? What do they want? Well, I suppose this is a way of keeping some people under control. How many—7,000? They told me that you police are responsible for this mess. I know—you're the police and they're the military—everyone tells stories about everyone else. But let's not worry about these accusations. My question is: "How can we find my passport here?"

Okay, Mr. García. I hope you're right. I'll see you at the counter in ten minutes.

What do you mean no Mr. Molinari works at this counter? I was just talking to him ten minutes ago. He suggested I look for my passport in the central room, but it's a mad house. Listen: a $10 million contract is dependant upon finding this passport. I am willing to pay whatever it takes to either find it or to get a new one. Can you do it for me? What do you mean I can't get a new passport? Who really cares if the computer says that I already have one! It's lost! Okay. Can you find my old passport, the one that was brought here? Who can I talk to? And where is this Captain Mazzi? Stay here. If he solves my problem, you'll get what I promised.

Is this the Blue Room? Mr. Portes sent me. He said my passport may be here. I'm Adelina Paz. Yes? Finally! Of course I'll come in . . . it's a complete mess downstairs. I was losing hope of finding my passport . . . What? What problem is there? Why? I've done nothing! There's nothing to interrogate me about. I'm leaving this place. What do you mean I'm under arrest? What are the charges? Can I at least call my lawyer? Why not? Where are you taking me in this elevator? Why? What have I done to be put in a cell? Of course I marched in May Square! I want my son and my husband back! . . . Let me out! . . . Somebody answer! . . . Let me out!

Yes—it's chaos. Captain Mazzi's office is on the third floor. I wish you well, but when I was there half an hour ago, he was quite unhelpful. I'm Ignacio José Conti, and your name is—? Gustavo Pereira—it sounds familiar. Yes. Pereira Manufacturing—I've seen the ads in the newspapers. Sure. These people are criminals. And they just keep blaming each other. The military upstairs say the police downstairs are creating this situation to get money. The police downstairs—who, by the way—take the money, say the military upstairs are creating the problems to keep the population under control. If you ask me, they're both telling the truth. But I must go. Good luck.

But Captain Mazzi, I have to sign a $10 million contract in Spain tomorrow! These people won't wait! You're ruining me and my company! Tomorrow! Everyone says tomorrow! It will be too late! Okay. This is my office telephone number. I'll be expecting your call.

Another hour has passed . . . No one has come . . . I'll never make it to France . . . I'll probably never make it out of here alive. Carlitos, Juan . . . I've failed you. Yet this may turn out to be the only way of being reunited. I love you both . . . I love you both . . .

He found it, he said. I still believe he knew it was there all along—in a box under his very own counter. I don't believe his claim that someone swept it there when cleaning the floors at night. At any rate, I've boarded the plane, and if everything goes well, I'll be back in the United States on schedule. I wonder what happened to Pereira—and to that small woman I saw admitted to the Blue Room.

I'm afraid I'll have to let you go, Irma. Without that contract, our firm is in serious trouble. Yes, we're broke. We'll have to shut down.

The pain from the rapes and the beatings . . . won't let me move and I don't want to move . . . Juan, dear Juan . . . Carlitos, my life's hope and happiness . . . We'll be together again, soon . . . when they shoot me out there, in the open fields, together with all of these other women they keep here . . . I love you both . . . I always have . . . Juan . . . Carlitos . . . I love you both . . .

SEPARATIONS

The Agony & Judgment of Ramón Reyes

I should have stayed with the goats! At least the air would have been cleaner. So many years of hard work in a thousand kitchens in this polluted city . . . and for what? I'm suffocating. There goes the doctor's shadow past the door again . . . I hate all this draining of my lungs, and living on borrowed time. An old windless windpipe . . . That's what I am! That's what I've always been . . . I wonder if I was ever a child . . . Maybe it all began with the goats, the mountains, and me as a young shepherd . . . But nothing begins for me any longer. My lungs have put hope and future behind me . . . If only I could have a smoke . . . A smoke! I want a smoke! I want to end it all in style! And now what? Everything is getting so dark . . . Whose hand is that? Whose body? Whose body is this, that looks like me, down there, on the humid sheets? No . . . I can't be dead! No! Not yet! Not with this pain in my lungs, this heaviness, this gasping for air, this nausea, this feeling of being disembodied and seeing my own corpse . . . I want this to be over! I want to die once and for all, without this hell, without this limbo . . . Death and nothingness are better than these scrapings of borrowed life . . .

"Who would have guessed. I thought he was going to survive all of us."

"I don't know, Ignacio. He always seemed sick to me. Remember his never-ending cough? It was no coincidence. He smoked those dark cigars all the time. And he knew it wasn't good for him, but he didn't care. It was as if something else, something deeper, was wrong with him. Otherwise, why would he keep on repeating, 'The only part of me that works is my stomach?' The fact is his entire body is failing now. And he's only sixty. What a life! I wonder whether he thinks it was all worth it. Listen! He's delirious again. What should we do? Will the doctor come back soon?"

"I'll see whether I can help him. Ramón . . . How do you feel? Would you like a sip of water?"

Why let all that milk drip from the four corners of this white room? Who's going to take care of it? Not Camilo. Nor Juana. Milk, not water. That's the problem . . . That's the problem . . . I want to sleep . . . Just for a while . . . Just for a while . . .

"He drank a bit and now seems to be resting, but he mentioned names I've never heard him mention before: Camilo, Juana. Does he have any family left?"

"I'm afraid that we Contis are the closest thing to a family for him. He has some distant relatives. Remember? Gramajo, the grammarian, who recommended the Spanish literature books Ramón was often reading and memorizing. And his cousins. But that's it, and he hasn't mentioned them for years."

"Why would anybody want to leave family and friends to go to a foreign land to work like a horse, stay poor, and die in solitude? Do you know why he came to America?"

"He once said he came because he disliked living in the small village in the Spanish province of León where he had been born. He took care of the family's goats. When he was 14, he was full of hopes and dreams, and tired of all of the goats, their smell, and the lack of alternatives. I understand him. Didn't I also leave family and friends to go to a foreign land where I worked like a horse and stayed poor? But I continue to pursue my hopes and dreams, and won't give up the search for freedom which led me to leave. What would be the alternative? Accepting failure? As for dying in solitude, the future will tell, but in a sense, we all do."

I am Fortunato Reyes . . . I have always been Fortunato Reyes . . . This is Fortunato's agony . . . But I cannot live as Fortunato, because as a minor, the governments of the world will not let me come to America of my own accord. I will fool them, though . . . I will cross the Atlantic pretending to be my brother, Ramón . . . I just use his passport, am identified as Ramón Reyes when I arrive at the harbor, and as such everyone knows me. I become my own brother . . . Yet, I am dying my own death . . .

"There he is—coughing and breathing heavily again. I'll go see."

The boat stinks . . . It stinks more than the goats . . . We are all sick . . . Two babies and an old woman die, their bodies soon to be food for the sharks . . . But the stench continues unabated. It's been going on for days . . . Desperation . . . But the ship's anchor is going down . . . What a sight from up here on the deck, crowded with hundreds of sweaty shoulders, immigrant shoulders like mine, seeing the Statue of Liberty . . . Yes! This is America! America at last . . .

"He's covered with sweat and mumbling something about stench, sharks, and America. Call the doctor, Marta. This may be the end."

And now what? The anchor is being lifted, and we are moving away from the land . . . What is happening? And the Statue of Liberty? To have seen it only to miss it forever! It's getting smaller . . . The torch light is getting dimmer . . . It's only a dim glimmer on the horizon . . . I think I can still see it . . . I won't let it go! No! I can't see it any longer . . . What cruel hoax is this? The disease? The Captain said what? They wouldn't let us disembark? And where are we going now? Cry! Cry, Fortunato, like all the others! Cry louder than the storm that surrounds us in this nightmare . . .

"The doctor said he will be here in an hour. In the meantime, the best we can do for Ramón is to make him comfortable."

Fifty days at sea . . . not knowing where we're going, surrounded by illness and death, rejected immigrants floating along the Americas' shores . . . Now, in the middle of the night, the anchor drops once again and we hear that this time, some country will take us . . . No one cares what country it is . . . We'll disembark in the morning, who knows where, to make a new life, who knows how . . . I wonder what language they speak . . .

"Ramón, Dr. Wolzman is here again to see you. Can you hear us? He's going to drain your lungs. This way you'll be able to breath better and get well soon. Come on in, Dr. Wolzman!"

There has been yellow fever and cholera in the land . . . They are vaccinating all of us. But why in the lungs? What do they know? They speak Spanish like Italians and know nothing about Spaniards . . . They call us all *gallegos* . . . as if we were all from the province of Galicia. So when one asked me whether I was a *gallego*, I said, "Yes. I'm a *gallego* from León." Ha! Everyone laughed but him! . . . Ouch! Those thousand needles hurt, deep inside the lungs, where no vaccine can work and no air can reach any longer . . .

"I doubt he can hear us, Marta. It may be better this way. He probably won't feel the pain either. Now please leave us alone. I'll be out in a few minutes."

I wonder who ever called this city Buenos Aires . . . good airs! What a name! It's always humid here. And who called this country Argentina . . . the Land of Silver? The silver is in Bolivia, not here . . . Everything is mixed up . . . Now in July, it's winter, not summer as it should be and is in mother Spain . . . and this is a nasty winter! A cold mist keeps on falling day and night and getting into our bones . . . An Englishman from the boat, who works at the slaughterhouse, says it's like London, but with more light . . . I hope this climate doesn't ruin my lungs. I'm beginning to miss the dry mountains of León . . . but not the goats. I'm going to make a fortune and leave . . . I have no doubt I'll be the wealthiest cook in Argentina . . . Then I'll be able to live where the air is cool and clear . . .

"How is Ramón doing, Dr. Wolzman? I'm so sorry to hear that. Would you like to have a cup of coffee? My sister Marta and I would like you to discuss the situation with our entire family. Our parents should be here soon. In fact, that's the doorbell. I think they're here."

I've worked as a cook in many restaurants, and have some money saved . . . You've been a waiter for years and have some money saved, too . . . Together, Antúnez, we can buy The Horse Races Bar and Restaurant, and make a bundle . . . What do you think?

"How are you, Dr. Wolzman? You know my wife, Josefina. Do you remember my brother, César? César, this is Dr. Wolzman, the best physician in the world, not only because he knows his trade, but because he's always there when you need him. What other physician would come to your house to take care of someone in the manner he has done?"

"I think, Colín, that we won't have to take care of Ramón for much longer. He's dying."

"I was afraid you were going to say that. Poor Ramón. How long do you think he has to live?"

"It's difficult to say. A few days—maybe a few hours. His lung cancer is well advanced and he doesn't seem to recognize anybody."

"Perhaps we should start getting in touch with a funeral parlor."

"That's a possibility. Though there are others. You could donate his body to science. As he once said, and you mentioned, Ramón has no family. If you, as his *de facto* guardian, signed a document saying you would like to donate his body to a university hospital, the legal procedure would cost you nothing. The university would pay the bill."

"But Ramón is still alive. Maybe we should talk about this later. Or can we ask him?"

"I'm afraid he's in no position to tell us; but you don't have to make a decision now. The earlier you start thinking about it, though, the less of a hurry there will be when his death is really upon us. Please let me know what you have decided as soon as you have done so. I can put the donation documents together."

"What will they do with the body?"

"The usual. It will be placed in a formaldehyde pool from which medical students would retrieve it to practice surgical procedures. After each practice session, it will be returned to the pool. As you know, it's crucial that the students learn by such practice. Having a new body available will be invaluable. For the bodies currently in the pool have been used so much that they are covered with sutures, and it's hard to practice on them. But now I must leave. Thank you for the coffee. Good night, everybody."

This terrible night with Lupa the whore will change my life . . . I just can't do it . . . She is laughing at me, calling me a sissy, and charging me for her wasted time anyway . . . Now I know that only my stomach works . . . Betting is a distraction and an opportunity to strike it rich. For the prospects of becoming the wealthiest cook in the country are becoming untenable . . . So I bet all my savings on the legs of a hundred horses: Penny Post, Yatasto, Brandy, and so many others . . . Sometimes I win; but mostly I lose . . . The result is that The Horse Races Bar and Restaurant won't be owned by Antúnez and Reyes anymore . . . I will sell my half of the partnership to Antúnez and then work there as a cook . . . Yes. I'm back to being just a cook, but I save my money, and one of these days I'm going to bet on a big winner . . . Indeed, I always pick the winners . . . What happens is that someone always changes my mind in the ticket line. But never again . . . Never again . . .

"Colín, I think that Dr. Wolzman is a vulture. He wants Ramón's body, not his health, and he wants it preserved in formaldehyde and abused by medical students for years!"

"Calm down, Josefina—please. What else can we do? Have him cremated?"

"I'm sure we can sign a document saying we want to bury him. Why wouldn't that work? Besides, cremation isn't right. It's certainly not right when it's done for the money. They cremated my father's body, but not because we wanted it. We couldn't pay for his grave. That's when the government got into the act. They never do it to help anyone, but to get a public nuisance out of the way—in this case, my father!"

"I don't think we should make this personal. Ramón is not your father. To be sure, he's almost like family to us, and we have treated him like family. He has no health insurance, and we've paid for the expense of keeping him home during his illness and having the doctor visit him here. As you know, burials are not cheap. Nor is it cheap to keep on paying for a grave. Frankly, I'm not sure we can afford this additional expense. As for his distant relatives, I called them but they have chosen to stay more distant than ever. What are we supposed to do? We've helped him while he's been alive. Why create a problem with his death? Marta, Ignacio, César—what do you think?"

"Brother, I think donating the corpse to science is not the worst alternative. After all, Ramón believed in science, especially in medicine. Remember? He used to quote the Spanish Nobel Prize winner for medicine, Ramón y Cajal, all the time. And didn't he give a copy of *The Tonics of the Will* to Ignacio for his 20th birthday? I have little doubt that had he been able to decide, Ramón would have chosen donation over cremation."

"How do we know, César? How do we know that? My father also believed in science. He was an amateur scientist himself, and he believed that people would go into space and eat pills rather than ordinary food someday. He died in 1912 from the pneumonia he got while cleaning his fish shop. I was only two years old. We paid for his grave until 1914. Then we couldn't afford it any longer and he was cremated. How could we have known if he would have preferred to have his body donated to science? It's all speculation."

"But mom, it's the best information we have. You can't expect to attain certainty on these matters."

"Maybe so—but it won't make me happy. You go ahead and do what you have to do. I just can't come to terms with it. Sometimes, the best information is not enough."

Fortunato . . . What a name I have for having been born so unfortunate . . . fifteen years have passed since I arrived in Argentina and now I live in an upstairs room of the restaurant I used to own . . .

I have no bed but the tile floor, where nearly every week I twist my arm when turning in my sleep . . . In such a condition, I can't even cook . . . Maybe Colín is right and I should move to the back room of his real estate company . . . I won't be rich, but I'll be all right . . .

"You should sign here, Mr. Conti. Thank you. In the event that Mr. Reyes dies, your physician will contact us to take care of all the formalities. Have a good day."

These canaries are sweet . . . I read they originally come from Spain, from the Canary Islands . . . But these have been born in captivity and are yellow, rather than green like the wild ones. I know they're not mine . . . I know I'm supposed to take care of them until Colín and his family return from their vacation . . . But I hope they'll always stay here and have children and grandchildren, despite my neighbor's opinion . . . What a witch Mrs. Ferrer is! I wish I didn't have to live in this back room together with all these other tenants! Garza the watchmaker has a temper, and so does his thin, 90-year-old aunt, María Puentes . . . Though they don't meddle with me, they fight and shout continuously in the kitchen we have to share . . . It's hard to cook, and impossible to sleep with these people, but at least they leave me alone . . . Mrs. Ferrer is a different story. Why won't the canaries reproduce? She shouldn't have meddled . . . "Ramón, don't waste your time; nothing is ever born in this house." Who does she think she is? What does she know? I'll show her . . . Catita, I just bought you to show the witch that this house is good enough for generations of canaries to be born in . . . Don't let me down . . . Go in. Go in, little bird . . . Meet your friends. They're canaries like you, even if not the same color . . . Go in. Go in, little one . . .

"Look, Josefina. César is right: Ramón respected science. Why wouldn't he donate his body to science if he was conscious?"

"How would you like it for your body to float in formaldehyde for years, until it's hardly recognizable from being pickled and sewn? Haven't you done this to save money?"

"No. Though as I told you, it's no minor matter that we would have to pay for the burial expenses on top of the medical expenses we have already incurred. I wish his distant relatives had not chosen to disappear when they heard that taking care of him was becoming expensive."

Chirp . . . Chirp . . . Hi, little canaries! Hi, Catita! Your little chicks are growing . . . Good! That will show the witch that it's possible to be born and live well in this house! I'll bring you fresh water . . . I'll be back . . .

"He was funny—"

"Don't talk in the past tense, please! He's not dead, yet!"

"But he's near death, mom, and he wasn't solemn about death. Remember the day he was coming back from the horse-racing track by train, and without a ticket because he'd lost all his money in the races? He saw the ticket inspector coming, got up and began walking towards the back of the train. The train was short and he soon made it to the end. The inspector kept on moving through the train, checking tickets and, eventually made it to the last car, where Ramón was trapped. But he was stubborn, and a man of many resources. Without hesitation, he jumped off through the back door. The train kept on going at about 40 or 50 kilometers an hour. Ramón was lucky to survive with only a few minor contusions. Some people who happened to be near the tracks brought him to the nearest hospital— where we went to pick him up. After telling us what had happened, he said, 'I was lucky to fall on my head; otherwise I'd have killed myself.' "

"Shhh! Here we are—telling funny stories about him while he's dying in the next room. This is beginning to look like a wake, where some people suffer, while others—who show up only as a matter of etiquette—socialize while having coffee and telling jokes. Have more respect for the dying!"

"I'm sure this is how he'd have wanted it."

Yes . . . I have a good memory. I can recite every work written by Cervantes, Quevedo, Góngora, and Lope de Vega . . . Gramajo lends me the books and I learn them by heart . . . However, you understand them. I don't. I have a dead mind. I've been dead since I left the mountains and the goats behind . . . Sure I talk . . . Sure I cook . . . Sure the food is good . . . but this is simply because the ingredients are good. The fact is, deep inside, I'm dead. I'm just bark . . . And I don't care about me . . . or anybody. But you, Ignacio, are going to study in the USA, where I tried to go and was rejected; but you're not me and will do well . . . Some people should try these things . . . Others, like me, should not . . . I wish I had not been born, but since I have, I can only wish to die soon . . .

"He was a good cook, but prone to accidents. Remember when the pastry exploded on him? There was oil splattered all over the walls and ceiling—which is quite high. Indeed, pieces of raw dough were hanging from the ceiling. Face down, he was mopping the floor. I asked him, 'What happened, Ramón?' He raised his face towards me. An enormous blister covered his entire forehead. He said, 'I thought I'd gone blind.' This was all I could get out of him. The man seemed to be in a trance. After asking again and again, he finally said, 'My pastry exploded. I had put it in the pan on the stove and all of a sudden, pieces began to jump all over the place. I ran to take the pan off the stove and they jumped on my face. It hurt and I could see nothing. I thought I had gone blind. Then I realized I had my glasses on and the dough had covered them.' Until this day, I do not know what was in the flour he used."

"I can hear him again. We should quiet down and let him rest."

Life goes on; but my life doesn't . . . I brought the canaries with me when I moved in with Colín and his family. These dear little birds have gone through many generations. Some, like Catita, died from old age. I wish I'd died instead . . . My lungs . . . they burn . . . but I wish I could have a smoke . . . Someone's hand pours water in my mouth . . . my insides burn . . . cancer and forgetfulness eat it all . . .

and the milk is dripping again from the four corners of this white room . . . Why does the door shrink as it does? I'll never be able to leave this way! Help! Fix the door! I have to go! And now those drops! The entire wall is covered with thick, white tear drops floating toward my bed . . . I feel nauseous . . . I can't breath . . . I have a vision that I'll return to the sea and float forever in the midst of hope! But that's no consolation. I should have never left the goats! It was all a mistake . . . It was all a mistake . . . The fluid . . . the fluid . . . takes over my lungs . . . and all that light! From nowhere and everywhere . . . From nowhere and everywhere . . . Fortunato Reyes . . . Ramón Reyes . . . Who was I? Who am I? What awaits me? All that whiteness! All that whiteness . . . and my corpse eternally floating in a quiet sea of hope . . . For . . .

Marcos Bardán

According to the Buenos Aires newspapers, my long-lost friend Ricardo Morales was found dead in downtown Buenos Aires just one week ago. His face had undergone a radical change, but his identity papers were with him, and initial tests identified him as who he was: Ricardo Morales.

I lost touch with him about twenty years ago, when confronted with the country's increasing military oppression, we both ceased to pursue our university studies in Argentina. I came to the United States in the wild hope of eventually becoming able to help my people from abroad, or if circumstances permitted, back in Argentina. Ricardo, more courageous or more impatient, joined the resistance. He went underground and I never heard from him again until I read the news of his death today. And I was barely beginning to recover from the emotional shock when I received a note from him in the mail, which I presume was written a short time before his death. It simply says: "Please read the enclosed. I can't go on without letting you know why you didn't hear from me during all these years. – Ricardo." And attached to this brief missive, I found a document with the following text:

> This morning at 10:00, Marcos Bardán assumed his position as Secretary of Labor. Bardán is a famous politician and union man, but his work in physics is utterly unknown. This work, however, was decisive in shaping his life and his political career. Hence, I shall

describe it here. Bardán studied engineering and physics at the National University of Buenos Aires. He left the university, and having assumed a false identity for political reasons, worked at a private physics lab for the next five years.

He was very interested in quantum physics. This led him again and again to perform a modified version of Schrödinger's experiment, which he found quite puzzling. Actually, his own version of the experiment obsessed him. Nearly every week, he would put a cat in a box, aim a loaded shotgun at the box, and connect the shotgun to an amplifier, which if activated, would fire the weapon. He wired this amplifier to a highly sensitive piece of lab equipment which could detect electrons. This in turn was attached to a single point on a surface of paraffin. He would place this surface behind another with two holes in it, and shoot an electron toward it. Sometimes, this electron struck the detector, the amplifier was activated, the shotgun fired, and a cat was killed by the discharge. Other times, the electron missed the connection, and the cat survived.

To Schrödinger, the experiment raised questions about the validity of quantum physics. To Bardán, it raised questions about the identity of particles, and indeed, of all physical objects. For according to one widely accepted interpretation of quantum physics, the physical reality of an electron striking the precise point on that paraffin surface (to which the electron detection equipment was attached) was only a set of probabilities. The probability of an electron striking that point, and of the electron striking a point one centimeter above it, and of another one a centimeter below it, as well as many others, all together described the exact place where the electron was. Each electron was at once in each and all of the places where it was probable that it would hit. The electron detection equipment, however, was wired to only one point. Therefore, each electron Bardán had shot, both had and had *not* hit the connection. Each time, then, the shotgun both had and had *not* been fired. And the cat was both dead and alive at the same time.

How could this be? Was the universe of physics merely a world of chance and contradiction? This implication was absurd. Yet, Bardán did not know what to believe. In the obstinate hope of finding out whether this wild possibility was indeed, a fact, one particular night he decided to do what he had done so many other times: to return to his laboratory and perform the experiment again.

A few cats were sleeping in cages piled up against one of the walls. Bardán looked at them from the door. One of the cats meowed, dreaming. Bardán went toward its cage, took the cat out, and put it in one of the boxes he used for this experiment. Sleepy, the cat searched for a comfortable position in its new bed. Bardán observed it for a moment. Then he shut the box. He began to shoot electrons at the paraffin surface. After two minutes, the shotgun went off. Bardán rushed toward the box. The door had been almost entirely destroyed by the discharge. Bardán opened what there was left of it and a perfectly healthy cat left its temporary prison with a jump, and hissing menacingly, scurried to hide behind a large bookcase. Astonished, Bardán wondered whether cats might not really have nine lives. He then looked into the box: another cat—identical to the former—lay inside, dead.

Bardán did not publish this result. He secretly kept on pursuing his research. But the logic, or the mere physics of the phenomenon, did not interest him any longer. The technology did. For if the phenomenon could be reproduced at will, it would obviously have very significant applications. One might, for example, develop a certain sort of immunity to armed attacks. And even if, strictly speaking, one could not develop any such immunity, the duplication of any individuals produced would certainly render these attacks pointless.

Soon afterwards, his facial features changed by a surgical operation, Bardán—or to use his real name—Ricardo Morales—changed his identity again, this time assuming the name by which he became famous, Marcos Bardán. He began to work in a metal plaque factory, and soon began to take part in political and union activities. He took part in many of the bloody demonstrations of that year. Ever since, his comrades called him "Nine Lives," because he was unhurt, even though the automatic weapons fire of the police often left a carpet of dead men around him.

Years passed. Bardán became Secretary of the Central Confederation of Labor. People respected him, but he was not happy. In fact, he began to become violently depressed. Finally, he committed suicide two years ago. Or rather, as he feared, he committed suicide and survived his own death. He became two identical persons—identical except one was dead, and the other alive. To cover this up, Bardán cremated his own body in a furnace at an abandoned factory. But he knew what had happened and was faced with his fate. His discovery had been fabulous. Its application was now irreversible—he could not die.

Bardán continued working for his country and its people, and living in a way that took account of his situation. But the awareness of his immortality took on a new significance for him. His point of view now changed. His urgency to create just social solutions diminished. His sympathy for the oppressed became more ambivalent. He could wait; but others could not. He was, in fact, condemned to wait for all eternity; while others had to struggle in the present. He lived in limbo; others lived in hell—but one that would end.

The President offered Bardán the Department of Labor. He accepted. This acceptance unleashed a grave political crisis. His enemies tried to assassinate him. At 7:00 this evening, he was shot in a bar across from the dark and imposing San Carlos Cathedral. In the skirmish, various individuals were killed. Bardán both was and was not with them. His corpse is now being viewed inside the office of the Metallurgical Workers Union. But he is alive. In any case, this is certain: Marcos Bardán is not qualified to be the Secretary of Labor. He is not qualified to live as a human being. For these reasons, through this letter, Marcos Bardán presents his irrevocable resignation from the position of Secretary of Labor that he assumed this morning. By the time this letter is received, he will be out of the country, and living under an assumed name—forever. Let the people understand.

—Marcos Bardán

South

Rather than a poem, it's a little song. Yes. I wrote it many years ago, during one of those cold autumns when I used to live almost in Canada. The birds had begun to migrate in unending flocks. Did you hear that some go as far as the southern tip of the Americas? I imagined them crossing the Amazon, and going along the Andes, wishing to see the pampas (like me). Nostalgic, I wrote the song. Its title is "*Sur.*" Yes. Of course. That's why. Carolina wrote the music for it, but when we broke up we stopped singing it together. Do you remember she mentioned it the last time she visited us? She had lost the music and we had both forgotten it. No. When am I going to write more poetry? This little song must be the last in the series. Poetry makes me nervous. No. What do you mean "translation"? Poetry cannot be translated. And as you can imagine, I don't know enough English to get myself involved in that. But you understand Spanish! What need would there be for me to translate it for you? If you want, I'll read it to you, but in my mother tongue. Besides, this way you'll practice. And especially this song—it would be treason to translate it. Here, it is really as they say: translator, traitor. But why? But why? I have to read it for you to see why. What do you mean it can't be treason? What do you mean it can't be that big of a deal? Of course it is! No, I'm not exaggerating at all! Do you believe that because you have lived with me for three years, you already know everything about me and my culture? See what I'm always telling you? You have a little closet for everything. But this country is unbelievable! And it must have stuck on you! It stuck when you were a kid. How do I know where? At school which, no offense, leaves much to desire, or at home, where your people were so many that there was no time to try to understand anyone. So I'm telling you again. Look before talking. And listen. Listen first and see whether I'm exaggerating. And where are you going now? What? I bet you got upset! Look at the expression on your face and you'll see why I'm saying it! And your tone. The tone that came into your voice! Metallic. Businesslike. What's the rush to suddenly wash clothes? There you go again. I told you a thousand times that love is not a contract, or 50-50, or even-Steven. And what proves it is the "You too, José! You too, José!" which after all isn't true because I don't budget my love like you do, nor do I keep on adding and subtracting to see whether you do or don't. And I'm telling you because I remember the thousand times that it turned out afterwards it was a fact that— Of course I'm shouting, not as in this regimented country where good people don't shout but with a calm voice and the economic pressure and the legal tricks and the "excuse me" if they sneeze; they give it to the Blacks and the Mexicans and the Puerto Ricans and to us, the foreigners, the smallest minority. And what is worse, when it concerns me, because my skin isn't brown or black and they believe I must be Italian. "I know you're not one of them," they tell me all friendly—like the guy at the diploma factory that time! What do you mean what do I want to do? There you go again. That you're not like that guy, that calling you a racist is to lie, that I'm more than exaggerating, and that the sneezing thing is only polite after all. Ah! Yeah, sure. I scare you because I get violent and you, visceral racist, because that's the kind of racist you are, you define violence as it suits you and as it turns out—oh surprise—I'm violent and scare you because I raise my voice even though I never touch a hair on anyone's head. And let me tell you that when you threw yourself on the ground in that parking lot—calling the police—it was all in your head and was all your theater. And you? Of course. How could you be violent if you don't raise your voice like us undeveloped people, even though with all that calm of yours, you stab me in the back as soon as I turn around! Of course, I suppose this doesn't count by definition. But look if you're not a racist, tell me what language we're speaking! What a coincidence! Even the fights are in English! And why do I always have to use *your* language? Simply because you, imperialist, need not worry about using mine? In what kind of melting pot are we living? In the one that melts me and shapes me into your image and likeness? What a sneak! Yeah, calm down, calm down. Racist! That's what you are! That's what you are and I'm shouting all I want! A thousand and one times I'm shouting it and so screw the neighbors, who are all that matters to you! What? Oh, that's what you were looking for! Oh yeah, you have a right to respect and either I treat you well or you leave, *et cetera*. And I in the meantime can't keep my dignity! But who put the crown on your head? Okay! Okay, madam! Sorry. Okay, Ms! *Piantáte* if you want to! There you go again. I know. I've heard it a million times. *Dije*, "Split! Take off! Go away if you want to!" Of course. As I always told you. See—you were going to do this in the end? I sang it to you. Or don't you remember? See how in the end you're dumping me? And just like that. As if it were no big deal. What's happened is you don't understand. What happens is you're an *angla*. But when are things going to sink in? You don't understand, I'm telling you. If you did, you wouldn't be doing what you're doing to me. But don't believe for a moment I'm going to drop on my knees begging you to stay. I also have my dignity—even though you never give a shit about it. If you want to go, then go. It's your decision. It's your decision, *carajo*—just don't put me in your little closet again! Yeah, lost perspective, lost perspective. I lost nothing. And you, what you have is the perspective of this damn country where everyone can talk and no one talks about anything worthwhile. Of course, they're good people! Who's saying they aren't? But go find greatness around here. You won't even see it in films. It's not the same. There you go with your little closet again. It's not the same I'm telling you! And don't ask me! I'm fed up with your questions! Yeah, sure. First you drive me crazy and then I'm supposed to explain what you don't understand—but staying calm. How can I stay calm, *carajo*, if I'm from nowhere? A transitory man. A resident alien everywhere. The citizen of nothingness. Shit. That's what I am. I'm telling you it's not the same. And quit asking me. I don't know how it is! It's been fifteen years since I left! How do you want me to know. Yes, I went back a few times, but always in   a rush and keeping a low profile so they didn't give it to me. I used to go back around Christmas, partly because the types with the Ford Falcons were busy celebrating and might not come after me as much as they might have other times. The country disappeared from under my feet. I know how it isn't, not how it is. Do you understand me once and for all? You, with your order and understanding of only what's utterly clear, and it turns out what's utterly clear is only what could happen here, in this ideal Anglo-Saxon world where you get mugged when you least expect it. But here is not there. I should have never left! And I should have never returned! I'm lost in memories here. I was lost in the unfamiliar back home. I'm equally cut off from life in both places. Yeah. It's easy to say that. It's easy to announce to the world, "I understand that these are different countries with different histories and different values." But that's an abstraction—a universe of closets! People there are kinder. They're not as competitive as here, where you have to be on guard all the time. The same thing again! See how you want to get me screwed and refuse to understand? It's impossible that you can do this again and again and again without realizing it. I didn't say people here are evil. I'm not ungrateful. This country may have helped me more than my own. And I acknowledge it. I came here to pursue my dreams of freedom and knowledge. Yes. I enjoyed the freedom and attained some knowledge. *And* we have much to learn here from the democratic ideals, though they sometimes aren't practiced much, and from science and technology, though they mainly use them to fight the Russians. Don't get confused. Those motherless types you mention are the military, the police, and some other evil sons of bitches! Most people are not like that! You believe they are because TV has brainwashed you about both my country and this "Great Democracy of the North." What? But do you really believe *que me vas a chamuyar, que la vas a arreglar con parla barata como de costumbre?* Sorry Miss, I'll make it perfectly clear in your English. I said: "Do you really believe that you'll fix this by giving me pre-packaged lines and speeches as usual? Ah! And it's me who—What do you mean no? Why not? Don't I even have the right to—Where has the freedom of the anti-Communist propaganda gone? What! Is there slavery again in this the land of Washington and Martin Luther King? You are leaving? Split, if you want to. But if you're going to, do it soon. *Chau!* Good bye, Miss America! Good bye, and don't ever come back. I'm going to read my little song to myself, alone as I ought to, and don't interrupt me. I'm busy.

Al Sur el destino.
Al Sur vuelve el tiempo,
la esperanza anida,
y todo es afín.

What are you staring at? Did you already pack the suitcase? Yeah, I'll send you everything, don't worry. And I'll pay the rent and whatever you want for the sake of the respect I need and will get only when I'm alone in this house. And listen to what I'm saying, so you see I have a conscience: If you want to stay here until you find an apartment, fine. I will sleep in the other room. I'm stepping aside. No spouse abuse here. I'll even help you find an apartment. Now what? But who can ever understand you? Or is it that—after all— you want me to go to a hotel? You women are all alike. When I'm leaving, that I should stay, and that you're leaving; when I'm staying, that I'm staying, and who do I think I am. Do as you please. I'll keep on reading my little song. Listen. Listen to the truth in this before you leave.

> *Pájaros tardíos*
> *cercados de inviernos:*
> *el alma oprimida*
> *y un afán: huír.*

Maybe in your confusion you struck the right chord. Maybe I should write poetry again. But of course, who cares? If I begin to write poetry—lonely like a dog and without any support or anyone who loves me— I'll end up in the insane asylum. What bothers me is that I've been living from one imagined extreme to another. I've gambled with my life—and lost. And you—you won't change! It's pointless to dream. I know you haven't suggested any change in plans and that you'll be out in no time! I know. But watch out! Don't even think of leaving that mess of panties and stockings which make the room look as if it had been decorated with banners. I still plan on living here. If you leave everything like that—because look: you're leaving me simply because I didn't translate that little song to you. I'm not saying anything else, but think about it. Because of a song I can translate for you any time. Do as you see fit. Leave if you want to. But don't go around saying I didn't make an effort. Of course I made it! Or are you blind? Look at that! I humiliate myself, I lose my dignity for us, and you don't even notice. What do I have to do? Tell me! What do I have to do for things to be good between us? I'm alone. That's what's happening. *Estoy solo como un hongo.* Not even God would be more alone if He existed with this merry-go-round world to bore Him and drive Him crazy. I'm a citizen of nowhere in a universe of closets. I can already see the end. I should have died as a little boy when they took out my appendix. Crazy or dead—this is my future. As my omen-song goes:

Final presentido
en dagas de hielo.
Memorias vencidas
y un afán: huír.

I'll translate it for you even if you don't care.

End foreboded
in daggers of ice.
Defeated memories
and an urge: to flee.

What a life of shit I've got! It's clear why you're leaving me. Because I'm worth nothing, and I'm nowhere. And you're right to leave. I'm finished. I can't stay, nor go back, nor go on. You can say what you want. Without you, I have nothing left. But what do you care. If you cared you wouldn't leave. Or aren't you leaving? You see? But how can you do this to me? Don't you understand? What happens is that I get depressed and exaggerate, *y me dá la viaraza.* I go crazy, Sue. *Yo no sé.* Poetry makes me nervous. Please, Sue. Please. *Escuchame.* Listen to me! I love you! I beg you! *Por favor.* Sue. Don't leave me. Sue. *No me dejes.* Please. Give me one more chance—

REVERBERATIONS

An Historical Problem

Tácito Romero has just died. His contributions to the history of the River Plate area need no recommendation. No accomplished historian doubts that they are the best on the subject. His posthumous work has not yet been published, but a few privileged historians have examined it. They found it fascinating, though often incomprehensible. Romero produced it during the last three years of his life. I had the good luck of being present at its inception.

One evening, during one of my recent visits to Argentina, Romero invited me to dinner in order to discuss a certain puzzling historiographical question. He wanted to hear the opinion of someone, who like myself, had a background in logic and the philosophy of science and was interested in ancient Greek philosophy. We went to a small, crowded restaurant in downtown Buenos Aires. Carried away by his enthusiasm, Romero didn't notice the crowd. Nor did I, after a short while.

He explained that his question concerned the work of Manuel García Sañudo, a historian of philosophy who had died the previous month. I knew very little about the man or his work. Romero told me what he knew. It was a great deal, because he had been closely acquainted with Sañudo and had read much of his work.

Manuel García Sañudo had suffered many academic defeats, but had never acknowledged any of them. He used to tell himself that serious scholars would someday discover his valuable contributions to the history of philosophy. This attitude made him especially fit for the unusual destiny which was awaiting him.

On a certain summer afternoon, while Buenos Aires was becoming drowsy under its gold and green trees, Sañudo walked through one of the city's parks without even noticing the sun, the heat, the humidity, or the intermittent relief provided by the occasional shade of those trees he passed under. A modest, more than 2,000-year-old question, a 50-year-old obstinacy, and an intellectual curiosity at its peak focused his vision inward rather than out. Only one issue occupied his mind. How could Aristotle have supported his observation that a body could be heavier under certain conditions than under others? With experiments? With theories? With other things? He stopped walking and recalled:

> "An inflated bladder is heavier than an empty one . . . A body . . . with more air than earth and water . . . does not rise in air, but it rises in water."
> (De Caelo, Book IV, 311b, 10-14).

What did scholars think of this? Some had thought that Aristotle neither had—nor could have had—any basis for asserting any such thing. Aristotle being the one involved, however, this interpretation was implausible. It was also unfair to hold it without reason. Others had thought that Aristotle had based his assertions about the light and the heavy on experiments with inflated bladders and empty ones. They'd thought that Aristotle had proceeded in accordance with the same empirical method that Galileo would use many centuries later to disprove Aristotelian physics. This opinion had no textual basis whatsoever, but it could be true—and it certainly was original— attributing to Aristotle, as it did, the use of the empirical method. Sañudo was both intrigued and disturbed.

Absorbed by his thoughts, he'd kept on walking around the park for hours. It was now getting dark. Sañudo, who had read absolutely everything written on the subject, made a drastic decision. This time, he was not going to run the risks of intellectual conservatism, but he was going to run all the others. He was not going to follow the rules of the community of historians because these rules did not serve to solve the problem with the certainty Sañudo was seeking. He was going to *re-live* Aristotle's reflections about the light and the heavy. He thought if he only succeeded in becoming sufficiently like Aristotle in the relevant respects, he would come to take the actual position of the Stagirite himself. The risk of intellectual expatriation was worth it when truth itself was at stake.

His task was immensely complex. And he was determined not to make it public. Were he to be successful at all, not just serious scholars—but geniuses—would be necessary to completely assess his contribution to the history of philosophy. There were, however, few geniuses around. For this reason, and because his search beyond the barriers of millennia was not going to appear urgent to other members of the scientific community, there was no hurry to let anyone know about his endeavor. He might at most mention it to a close friend or two. Why worry about immediate public recognition anyway? What mattered to him was the truth. He fanatically believed that even the most modest truth was worth any sacrifice.

The one that was consuming him now had to do with the roots of a way of thinking and living in which many others, and no doubt Sañudo himself, had been formed. To search for this was certainly worth the indefinite postponement of any recognition by the public or the established historians of his time. Taking slow steps, he went home and began to work on his project.

Years passed by, but Sañudo did not exhibit many noticeable changes. However, he developed a tendency to spend long solitary hours in the city's squares, walking around them or sitting on their benches, and never published anything else. His colleagues became accustomed to his introversion. His students found him correct, precise, and exhaustive, but more and more distant. Neither his wife nor his few acquaintances reported any remarkable change in his behavior. One day he retired, and no one heard of him until his death. Manuel García Sañudo died three years ago, leaving a massive and detailed kaleidoscopic work titled *On the Light and the Heavy* unpublished. In a short preface, the author describes his aim and the circumstances in which he decided to write his work. In what follows, every known and many an unknown interpretation of the Aristotelian text is put forward as *the* true theory about the light and the heavy. In each section, the name of the author is "Aristotle." No section of the work appears to be incomplete. Nor does Sañudo appear to have abandoned the project at any time. In fact, he was found dead, sitting at his desk, leaning on his copy of the traditional *On the Light and the Heavy* opened to the last page.

This is everything Romero knew. The story fascinated me. How were Sañudo's writings to be interpreted? As his behavior indicated, he did not appear to have gone mad despite the desperate character of his intellectual expatriation. Nor did he believe his posthumous work to be a failure. Had he believed this, he would not have continued his work after the first couple of sections. Instead, judging by the position in which his body was found, and by his widow's reports, Sañudo appears to have kept on working on his project right up to the moment of his death. Had he then been successful? If so, what had he discovered?

Encouraged by the wine and the meal, and perhaps by our own experiences as expatriates of one type or another, Tácito Romero and I concluded that there was only one way to interpret Sañudo's results correctly—to *re-live* his experience. We thought that if one became sufficiently like him in the relevant respects, one would come to understand his statements exactly as Sañudo meant them. When we agreed to this, we had already finished dinner and were walking in the park. We suddenly felt very tired, and soon parted.

Time passed. I continued to devote myself to logic and possible worlds, and to work on my monograph about Plutarch's *Parallel Lives*, projects that the distance, the lack of communication, and the cultural changes in my environment did not appear to hinder. More passionate than me, Romero moved into the house where Sañudo had lived until his death. Soon afterwards, he married Sañudo's widow. His enthusiasm never seemed to cease; but his communicability did. Then the sudden news came: he and his wife had died in an automobile accident about a month ago. I, given the recent moves toward democracy in Argentina, have returned to the country and have now moved into the house they used to live in. This letter is to let you know that my previous house is now ready for you.

—Ignacio José Conti

DÉJÀ VU, Richard Kendrick
353 pages $15

ISBN-10: 0-9755716-0-5
ISBN-13: 978-0-9755716-0-6

. . . full of lyrical descriptions of far off lands yet hits home with absolute poignance; it presents the world in a prism of adventure and experimentation, so much so that it reminds one of the enduring spirit of American literature. Kendrick revives Melville, Twain, and Kerouac in a voice that openly rejects the conventions of today, even as it demands fresh perspective. The book is essentially a search for truth; its form is unique and inventive, based upon the cyclical nature of time, subjectivity and the concept of fulfillment. I recommend it to everyone tired of the monotony of an everyday performance without avail, to you who lust for travel! -- *Lucas Hunt*

A rare book that combines modernist formal experimentation with excellent post-modernist content and prose; this novel is as much about form as it is about plot. Part *bildungsroman* part travelogue, both funny and serious, a blend of facts, fictions, and dreams; Déjà Vu . . . risks comparison with novels like Cortázar's *Hopscotch* and Perec's *Life: a User's Manual* (I generally don't like to use the word "risk" in art criticism, but I think it's appropriate here) and I think it stands up very well. Saying that I actually preferred this to either of them would sound pretentious; but . . . the content of this novel is more to my liking than that of the others. -- *Rick Russo*

CODE GREEN, Greg Jenkins
227 pages $15

ISBN-10: 0-9755716-1-3
ISBN-13: 978-0-9755716-1-3

Chip Stone is a male nurse who works in a psychiatric hospital and has almost as many behavioral issues as the residents he cares for. These include DeWitt, a cultural critic gone bonkers; Tim Valentine, who snacks on light bulbs; Philip Nolan, who contends (correctly) that he's a character in a book; and Glinda Moon, an anorexic witch. As the violence at his workplace intensifies, the confused Stone sets out on a desperate but comical odyssey to find his estranged wife–and himself. His wanderings take him through a twisted netherworld where he meets old friends, new enemies and one highly unusual sister-in-law. He discovers that the line between the sane and the not-so-sane is more gossamer than even he had suspected. With over-the-top characters and gaudy, entertaining prose, this engaging work offers a bumptious blend of humor and pathos well-suited to the uncertainties of the new millennium.

LIVES, Lucas Hunt
93 pages $10

ISBN-10: 0-9755716-2-1
ISBN-13: 978-0-9755716-2-0

A rich and lyrical collection of poems - both a passionate and occasionally ironical account of life in a modern world of infinite possibility. Here is the full spectrum of the varied colors of human experience from the pleasantly erotic to the disturbingly violent. The poet breaks from contemporary forms of expression to confront reality and the beyond, and to communicate powerful truths about eternal situations. With vivid (and visceral) imagery of work, love, dreams, and death, these poems celebrate the phenomenal aspects of life while acknowledging the futility of our continual search for meaning. The need for ritual, reason, and intoxication all serve as (black) comic relief from the all-too-common experience of tragedy.

If ordering directly from Vagabond Press, add $3 postage and handling per order.
Vagabond Press, PO Box 4830, Austin, TX 78765

More essential fiction from Vagabond Press

Déjà Vu
Richard Kendrick

ISBN 0-9755716-0-5
352 pages
$15.00 (paper)

If ordering directly from
Vagabond Press, add $3
postage and handling
per order.

VAGABOND PRESS
PO Box 4830
Austin, TX 78765
vagabondpress.com

Alden Homer and Blake Whitman are traveling their own paths, which seem to cross more frequently than usual for a couple of dissimilar guys on the road in Asia. Their thoughts and experiences are pieces of a puzzle that the reader can assemble, as this seminal work allows the reader to participate in the construction of the narrative.

Alden, who experimented with drugs during his Ivy League days, is now in his 50s. He has passed through Wall Street and sacrificed a marriage to his literary aspirations. Searching for the Muse, he'll settle for enlightenment. Blake is taking a year off before medical school, and is enthusiastically seeking the adventure he could only read about—or see in the movies— back home in Middle America. He chases the Exotic. Independently or together, these two colorful characters encounter a nymphomaniac, a murder victim, Christian fundamentalists, Hindu holy men, inmates at a mental institution, and a yeti - not to mention their own dreams.